HOT OFF THE PRESS

A Lesbian Romance Novel

AUTUMN WOLFF

Copyright © 2024 by Autumn Wolff

This is a work of fiction. Names, characters, business, events and incidents are the products of the author's imagination. Any resemblance to actual persons, living or dead, or actual events is purely coincidental.

Cover design by CloverPatchMouse

The scanning, uploading, and distribution of this book without permission is a theft of the author's intellectual property. If you would like permission to use material from the book (other than for review purposes), please contact autumnwolff4@gmail.com. Thanks for supporting the author's rights.

First print edition: August 2024

This book is dedicated to my amazing wife, Meghan, who passionately supports all the wild words I slap down on the page. It's also dedicated to Arra, Soph, and Issy who cheered me on through every chapter.

(Frankie)

"My answer remains the same, Mr. Cutlow. I'm not selling the paper. It's been in my family for three generations, and it'll stay that way," I said, blowing the bangs out of my eyes again. What was that? The fifth time during this phone call?

"Ms. Ricci, I don't think you'll find a better offer than what I've sent you today," Mr. Cutlow said, probably reclining at his desk in a Manhattan office overlooking one of the more famous avenues.

I rubbed the bridge of my nose as a light knock at the door pulled my focus away from the infuriating man. I was getting tired of being polite. This was the fourth offer for my newspaper I'd received this year from Aidan Global Capital. They were doing their best to scoop up the few remaining dailies in Maine, and I just wasn't having it.

The squeaky door cracked open slowly, and a man twice my age and half my hair length peeked inside. His face was scrunched in pity like he was watching someone sitting in a dentist's chair, a place I'd almost rather be.

He eyed me with a cautious look that let me know something more important than Mr. Cutlow needed my attention.

"Fortunately, Mr. Cutlow, I don't need a better offer. The Portland Lighthouse-Journal isn't for sale. Thank you for your time, but I have a news meeting to run. Have a nice day, bub."

Without waiting for his protest, I hung up the dated yellow-stained phone.

"Another offer gone all stove up to hell?" the man standing in my doorway said with a snicker.

I grinned.

"You know it, Richard. Watcha need?"

"My editorial for the Sunday paper is all set if you want to give it the once over," he said.

Richard was a large man who was never seen without baggy tan pants, a brown belt, and a striped button-down shirt. The top of his head was almost bare, but he still kept a ponytail about half the length of mine on the back of his scalp.

He wore boxy black glasses that made his eyes look bigger.

"Sounds good. Is it in GPS?"

"Yeah. The slug is 'unhousedED'," he said, turning to go.

I sat back down to my Macbook Pro, which was at least 10 years outdated and still chugging along with bubble gum, tin foil, and whatever else our IT person could cram inside to get a few more days of service from it.

Finding the article right where Richard said it'd be, I took a deep breath and remembered our last editorial meeting that'd nearly devolved into a shouting match between Londa, our Features Editor, and Richard, our Opinion Editor. Our Publisher, Franky Jr. (or papà at the family dinner table), was rubbing his head and trying to keep his blood pressure low like the doctor told him at every appointment. And I had to play referee as I so often did.

My eyes scanned the article and brushed over words like "affordable housing," "rehab," and "clearing camps," terms that always seemed to show up when the topic of unhoused folks in Portland was being discussed. It was an increasingly common topic over the last few years.

I read the article silently and then pulled the laptop onto my legs as I leaned back into my brown leather office chair. It squeaked even louder than my door. My reporters and editors often joked they knew I was in the office by two signs.

First, I never left the newsroom. It was my home, and I was always here.

Second, my chair squeaking could be heard all the way on the other side of the office. Ghost even heard it in the IT room if the police scanner wasn't too noisy.

My green lamp flickered, and I sighed.

"Hang in there, little bulb. The office supplies arrive tomorrow. . . I think," I said. For all the bluster I carried when rejecting Mr. Cutlow's offers to buy my newspaper, it wasn't like we were in a good spot financially.

Reading the editorial aloud in a whisper, I went through it again. Richard laid the groundwork for our stance on a new city ordinance that would be voted on next Tuesday, giving the Portland Parks Department and Health and Human Services Department the joint authority to declare a camp of unhoused individuals unsanitary and clear it.

The editorial noted that our city just opened a new shelter in North Deering, and it had enough beds to provide adequate space for unhoused individuals throughout the city. And the North Deering shelter opened just two months after a separate shelter for asylum-seeking families was finished in Bayside. Neither project would have been possible without state and federal grants. And neither was enough to solve the city's issues.

"Welcome to Portland," I muttered. "Where the only thing more plentiful than Massholes are short-term rentals."

Clearing my throat, I came to one of the last sentences and continued reading it aloud, "It's imperative that the Legislature continue to examine our city's shelter needs and increase funding for all the people other Maine towns don't want to house as they send them here instead."

That probably needs to be reworked a little, but the rest of the article is good, I thought, making a few notes in an email for Richard.

My phone chimed with a calendar notification that said, "Book Club."

"Oh shit! How is it already 7?" I groaned, getting out of my chair and grabbing my long black jacket from the door. Late April in southern Maine meant it might be nice and sunny during the day, maybe even warmish as winter slowly receded, and mud season started to gradually pull in spring. But as the sun went down, it'd get chilly again.

I closed my laptop, shut off my flickering lamp, and closed the office door behind me as I stomped into the newsroom.

Three rows of computers and desks sat half-filled, the result of voluntary buyouts and a round of layoffs. My feet traipsed over a thin gray carpet that was here when my grandfather started the Lighthouse-Journal. The smell of cigarette smoke and burnt coffee filled the newsroom, and somehow I never went nose blind to the scents. Then again, I didn't want to. They were home.

Our sports editor, a Latina baseball superfan named Isabelle, flagged me down before I'd made it halfway to the exit. She had a signed Boston Blue Sox ball sitting in a glass case beside her monitor.

"Hey Frankie, I've got a profile on Portland

High School's new men's basketball coach, but the superintendent is asking that we wait until the official announcement this weekend before we publish the story. How do you want to handle that?"

"He's the guy from Vermont, right? The one you confirmed with two different sources?"

Isabelle nodded, her golden earrings occasionally poking out of her short brown hair when she moved her head just right.

"Do any of the TV stations have the story yet?"

My sports editor scoffed.

"The TV stations hardly touch sports. Channel 7 only shows up for Sea Pups games on opening day. Channel 9 has more stories about Boston sports than Portland games. And I'm not even sure Channel 14 even runs sports stories anymore. I'm pretty sure all their corporate owners determined local sports coverage wasn't profitable enough," she said, putting hands on her hips.

I nodded. That checked out, actually. I didn't watch the TV stations very often, but I couldn't recall the last time I saw a story that wasn't about Boston sports on any of them.

"The superintendent uses a lot of executive sessions for his school board meetings. If I'm being honest, he's a pain in the ass, and I doubt he'll stick around for more than another year or two," I said, rubbing my chin.

Isabelle smiled. She knew where I was going.

"Fuck him. Run the piece whenever you want," I said, turning to leave.

The sound of our police scanner perked my ears, officers responding to a shooting on Forest Avenue. I turned to our evening city editor, a recent hire from Houston. Her curly red hair was pulled back into space buns, and a cute sweater covered most of her creamy skin.

"Already on it. I'm texting the PIO now," she said.

"Thanks, Emma," I said.

We'd hired her a few months ago, our first trans editor here at the paper. She'd been looking for a way out of her home state that was increasingly working to make her life hell. I liked Emma. She didn't complain about working the late shift, her copy was always clean, and she knew the cops and courts like the back of her hand. I tried not to hold her broadcast background against her but teased her about it occasionally.

"I'm surprised to see you leaving before 9 p.m.," Emma said, looking at her phone while she texted Sgt. Banks with the Portland Police Department.

"Hey, Radio Girl, you can give me shit about my hours when you've been here longer than six months. Until then, you keep your remarks quiet, or I'll throw you at the Portland Public Radio news-room. Their managing editor is twice as scary as me, and I'm pretty sure he reads those wizard books you hate at least twice a year."

"Holy shit, Frankie. I hope wherever you're going has tranquilizers and comfy blankets," she said, raising an eyebrow and grinning.

I shook my head, fighting a laugh.

"Just track down that shooting. Send Craig over if it turns into something, and there's still a scene," I said.

Walking outside into chillier air than I expected (wasn't it 60 earlier today?), I pulled out my earbuds as a firetruck went by, sirens blaring.

Looking behind me to make sure no one in the office needed anything, I popped my shoulders and started walking down Congress Street.

Behind me, the Portland Observatory stood tall, plunging most of my side of the street into shadow. Our newsroom sat in a blue shack next to the defunct marine signal tower shaped to look like a lighthouse. It was 86 feet tall and stood as a beautiful piece of marine history, seated right here in Munjoy Hill.

I pictured Dad carrying a younger me on his shoulders as we stood next to the outside railing at the very top, overlooking Portland's harbor, as well as the rest of the city I'd called home for all 30 years of my life. Seagulls screaming obscenities as they flew by, hunting for a scrap of trash to fight over, the smell of low tide (an acquired taste), and if you were lucky, a port full of sailboats, Casco Bay ferries, and cargo ships filling the water from the harbor out to Fort Gorges. Back then, I could sit up there for hours and just look at the water, but Dad's shoulders would get tired, or someone from the newsroom would page him.

Even now, I still hear him asking, "Did I ever tell you the story of how your great-great grandfather paid Captain Moody $5 every year to use this very tower and keep an eye on competing ships entering the harbor?"

When I was little, I loved the story. I had every word memorized by the age of nine. As a teenager, I rolled my eyes when he'd tell it during one of our many visits to the observatory. And in my 20s, I just started smiling and appreciating the story for what it was, his way of reminding me our family had called this city home for centuries. And God willing, we'd continue to for as long as we could. . . if these goddamn "luxury" real estate developers didn't push us out of Portland first.

I scrolled on my phone until I found the audio-book I was supposed to finish last night. If I hadn't gotten a call from a legislator who was pissed about a piece we ran on his speeding tickets, I'd have finished the book. Instead, I argued with the lawmaker for an hour about how his speeding tickets were public knowledge and in the public interest for us to report on. I sent him links to stories we'd written about lawmakers from both sides of the aisle when they had a brush with law enforcement.

Neither of us was happy when the call finally ended, a staple of my job.

It'd be about a 20-minute walk to the brewery the book club was meeting at, and I had just that much time left in the final chapter.

The book we were reading this month was a creepy vampire-ish novel called *House of Hunger*. I'd enjoyed it so far, but the last few chapters had been a roller coaster that left me breathless.

Just before I got my other earbud in, a man in a tattered gray jacket pushing a shopping cart stopped in front of me. His face was unshaven, and one of his eyes was covered with a scar or two.

"Ma'am, can you spare a couple of bucks so I can grab something to eat?"

I made eye contact with the man before speaking.

"I'm sorry, I don't have any cash on me right now," I said, a rehearsed line I used at least a few times a week.

"Yeah, okay," he muttered before continuing on down the road toward Monument Square.

When was the last time I carried cash? I thought, frowning. *Right. Weed store. How do they still not take debit cards in the year of our Lord 2024?*

I walked down the hill and turned onto Washington Ave, all the while mentally screaming at Marion to run! Just run!

My heart was thumping hard as I made my way

to a brewery called Portland Craft Distilling. It was a gray brick building with an entrance in the back.

I finished the book just before I walked inside, wiping some sweat from my forehead. The brewery wasn't packed. A few couples sat here and there with drinks, chatting about their day. On a little stage by the entrance, two men with acoustic guitars were doing a sound check. It made me wonder how we'd talk about the book with them playing in the background.

Large wooden tables and metal stools separated me from the bar. I wandered over, and the bartender, a man named Chris, asked if I wanted to order something.

I asked for a cider and some chips and salsa after looking at the menu.

"Do you know if a book club is meeting here tonight?" I asked, scratching my arm. This was supposed to be my first meeting, and I'd checked the location three times this afternoon like it might suddenly vanish into an alternate dimension if I didn't keep a close eye on it.

Chris finished pouring a beer and smiled at me.

"The book club? It's meeting in the Barrel Room, back through those doors behind the stage. It should be quiet enough that none of you will hear the music," he said as I handed him my debit card.

I peeked back into the Barrel Room, and nobody was there yet. So, I decided to sit at the bar for a few minutes, not wanting it to be too obvious that I was the first to arrive at the meeting. I emailed one of the book club leaders a couple of weeks ago, asking if they were still taking members.

A bubbly woman named Diana had responded and told me, "Of course!" She informed me what they were reading this month and gave me the time and place for the next meeting.

The brewery was getting a little louder as a large group of men in leather jackets came in. I raised an eyebrow.

Guess they're here for the music, I thought, sipping on my blackberry cider.

I turned back to my phone, checked my work emails, and saw the city had responded to a FOIA request I sent last week. Before I could read their response, a woman took the seat next to mine and plopped a book down on the bar, the very book I'd just finished listening to minutes ago.

Looking up, I found the prettiest girl I'd seen perhaps in all my life staring back at me. She wore a purple bandana covering her short curly brown hair and green eyes that seemed to smile at me. Her lips were painted a soft pink to match her eyeshadow.

A nosering in the shape of a little goat hung from her right nostril. Her pale skin had a few freckles on each cheek.

She smoothed her emerald wrap dress that complimented her eyes, and in a warm smoky voice asked, "Can I help you?"

My new friend at the bar didn't sound angry or annoyed at my staring. The way her lips curled at the end, she almost seemed amused.

"I, uh, your book. Yes! I was staring at your book," I said, finding my tongue tied now of all times. Arguing with a state senator? Child's play. Talking to pretty girls at the bar? A lyrical labyrinth full of land mines.

She chuckled.

"Well, my book is on the counter. And your eyes were. . . more in this area," she said, circling her face with a couple of fingers.

My cheeks burned.

"Sorry. I'm waiting for this book club to start, and I'm a little nervous. I've never been in a book club before," I said, scratching my arm again.

"Well, you're in luck. I'm also here for the book club. I was just going to order a drink before heading into the back room. You can wait with me if you want. But if you continue staring, I'm gonna have you buy my drink."

I nearly choked on my spit.

Clearing my throat, I said, "Sorry about that. I'm Frankie Dee, by the way."

"Dawn Summers," she said, looking at the drink menu.

I just sat there awkwardly, trying to look anywhere other than at the pretty brunette to my left. My eyes decided to take a new sudden interest in an empty table. It was an amazing piece of lumber. Was it pine? I wondered if it had a cool story. My brain imagined an entire backstory for this single table while I waited for the bartender to get Dawn a Long Island iced tea.

She touched my arm, which sent a jolt of electricity straight to my core.

"You can stop staring at the table now. I've already paid for my drink," she said as we moved toward the Barrel Room, and I prayed to God that my tongue wouldn't trip over itself for the next hour.

2

(Dawn)

The Barrel Room was aptly named. It was literally a room full of shelves holding large wooden whiskey barrels. From the floor to the ceiling, it was nothing but barrels. There were more than enough here to smuggle all the dwarves out of Mirkwood.

In the center of the room, a long corporate-looking table waited for us. This looked like something right out of a boardroom. It could comfortably seat about 20 folks, but I'd wager Diana would find a way to squeeze in more chairs for 25 ladies eager to discuss their latest communal read.

I walked over to the table's left end and sat near one of the corners. My new friend followed quietly, looking like a bashful creature. Gods she was cute. Her long blonde hair was pulled back into a high ponytail, and her brown eyes kept looking every which way as she tried to avoid staring at me, another endearing quality.

She must have come straight from work because Frankie Dee was dressed in a blue button-down shirt and tight black pants. I wasn't sure how my new friend managed to keep her fair skin so tanned during the winter, but she found a way.

Frankie looked like she was wound tight enough to snap, and I wondered what kind of life she led that twisted her up so much. She couldn't have been but a few years older than me, but she already had the age lines of someone in their mid-to-late 40s.

I sipped my tea, and she did the same with her drink.

Trying to ease up on the flirting and tension so thick not even a knife could cut through it, I turned my attention to the room.

"Wow, it really smells like whiskey in here. I don't know if I'll even go nose blind to it," I said, looking at all the shelves.

Frankie Dee's eyes trailed mine before she spoke again.

"Honestly? This place seems like it should be a gentlemen's club where they smoke cigars and play cards," she said.

I snickered.

"The kind of place where they'd call you a 'nosy dame' and tell you to 'beat it'?" I offered.

"Yes! Exactly that vibe," Frankie said, sipping her drink.

A woman wearing a blue puffy coat and leggings walked into the room carrying a hardbound cover of *House of Hunger*. Her hair was dyed blue and shaved on one side.

"Hey there, Dawn! I feel like I haven't seen you in forever," she said with an airy voice.

I smiled and stood up to hug Diana, the founder of our little book club that she'd dubbed the Casco Book Coven.

"But I also feel like I see you all the time because I hear your podcast every morning. It's a strange feeling," she said, setting her book down as her candy cane earrings jingled.

Taking another drink, I grinned as we sat down.

"Well, I guess I'm just glad you still listen. You were one of my first Patreon subscribers, ya know?"

"Oh, that's right! Back in 2018, the before times," she said, laughing. "Shit. That feels like ages ago."

It really did. Before the pandemic, starting my own witchy business seemed like a terrible idea. But when you're working a minimum wage retail job for years on end, you quickly find that you don't really have much to lose.

When I closed my eyes, I could still picture my first setup. I scraped together enough money to buy a decent little microphone. It was the ugliest bulb of a mic, but it had good reviews and surprising sound quality. It was the last one at Best Buy, which I saw as a sign.

I crammed myself into the closet with a little stool and bedside table, my laptop screen providing the only light. It was a hoot, let me tell you. The first couple of years were hard as I struggled to build an audience.

I vividly remember crying over my Audacity projects, eyes sore from staring at the screen for so long, wondering what the point even was. I'd spend the whole day dealing with shitty people behind the register at a dying clothing store that shall not be named. And then I'd come home, throw a Hot Pocket in the oven, light some incense on my altar to The Morrigan, and start editing audio.

Then Covid happened, and the world went to shit. Suddenly an astrology podcast was a hit. People somehow found Dawn's Divinations and subscribed in droves. Things took off so quickly, I told my handsy manager to fuck off and could even afford some artists to make merch like stickers and keychains my listeners were eager to buy.

"Oh! Before I forget, this is Frankie Dee, our newest member," I said, motioning to the woman who had taken advantage of our conversation to scarf down a plate of chips and salsa that were brought in by a server.

When the plate came in, it was full of red, black, and brown tortilla chips. And somehow, in the span of maybe 60 seconds, half of that plate had emptied.

Damn, she eats fast, I thought.

"Thank you so much for opening a space for

me. I've. . . never been part of a book club before," Frankie said.

"Of course! Welcome. How do you like to read?" Diana asked. And I shook my head. She asked this question of all new book club members like it was the most fascinating piece of information she could get.

"Oh, um, audiobooks, I guess? I don't have a lot of time because of work, so I have to listen if I want to finish any books," the hungry blonde said, eyes sneaking glances back down at her chips and salsa. I'd wager she was silently wishing Diana would stop talking to her so she could finish that plate.

This poor thing looks like she hasn't eaten all day, I thought, raising an eyebrow.

Diana nodded as a few more girls and a couple of thembies piled into the room. Some were carrying the book. One or two had their Kindles with them.

"I'm all about my little Nook. I use it so much the battery wore out, and I had to get it replaced" Diana said.

Pulling Diana's attention back to me, I asked, "How much did that cost? Because I didn't think they sold spare batteries for those."

She rolled her eyes and turned to face the only witch in the room.

"Oh, they don't! I had to have an electronics repair guy do it. Cost me more than a new tablet would have," she said.

I raised an eyebrow and saw Frankie devouring her remaining chips and salsa while our club leader was distracted. Fighting to keep my grin from showing, I listened to Diana talk about how much she loved her little tablet she'd affectionately named Nookelback while a themby named Ginger brought in a few more chairs.

Frankie's plate was cleared, and her glass was empty by the time Diana started the meeting, and we went around the table sharing our names and pronouns.

"Okay, so what did we think about the romance in this story?" Diana asked.

A girl named Jessica blurted out, "She was so awful! I hated how Lisavet treated Marion."

Ginger shrugged and said, "What can I say? I love a good bloodthirsty woman. And I think she really did care about Marion in the end, with the diamond and everything."

I leaned forward and said, "I'll second that. I love when women."

The room dissolved into laughter.

At one point, I noticed Frankie hadn't chimed in yet. And Diana must have as well because she turned to her and asked, "So what did our club's resident newbie think of the ending?"

Suddenly, the girl sitting beside me wasn't so shy.

"I found the ending pretty cathartic. The story starts with a long journey on a train and ends with one. I'm not sure I could have asked for a more satisfying conclusion."

I nodded, and Frankie seemed to lose her words when she finally turned toward me, putting her hands in her lap and sitting back in her chair all tight once more.

Diana left the room to get a refill, and a woman named Jackie sitting at the opposite corner of me said, "I just wish we'd gotten a little epilogue with a time skip at the end, you know? I wanted to see how she settled into her new life and how the other girls handled the transition."

A few people agreed, but I shook my head.

"I think the story ending on the train is exactly what I wanted. My favorite books are those that draw to a close just before the narrative seals itself airtight," I said, finishing my drink. "I like it when there's enough space left in the story to imagine what might happen next."

Frankie Dee was staring at me again, her eyes mesmerized while I talked about my literary preferences. So I turned to her and whispered, "Congratulations. You've just bought my next drink."

Her cheeks flushed as she coughed and squirmed in her chair. But in the end, she merely said, "Uh huh. . ." and left to get that refill.

She's fucking adorable, I thought, picturing the tarot pull I'd done after recording this morning's episode.

The Two of Cups practically jumped out of my

deck and into my hand when I finished shuffling. And I found myself visualizing the card in my hand. The deck I used most frequently and kept on my altar to The Morrigan was called Wise Goat Tarot. All of the cards featured goats of different colors, poses, and sizes.

In The Two of Cups I'd drawn today, I found two brown and white goats rubbing heads together, with a golden chalice covering one horn on each animal. It looked like each of them had stuck a curved horn into the chalice and then picked it up, wearing it as a tiny hat.

The card represented the connection between souls and a joyous spontaneity that came along with it.

And when Frankie Dee brought me back a new Long Island iced tea, I couldn't help but find myself wanting to flirt with her some more. I was feeling spontaneous and wanted to see if I could unwind the tightly kept woman who stumbled into my path tonight.

Maybe I'd even share some of my lipstick with her if things went well. Because tarot pull or not, there was one thing I was sure of about Frankie Dee. She may be straightforward (when she's not going gaga staring at me), but she is most definitely not straight.

⬒

"OKAY, remember for next month's meeting we're reading The Moth Keeper by K. O'Neill," Diana said.

Ginger smiled and said, "Excellent. My plan to get everyone obsessed with my favorite Kiwi author is progressing nicely."

I snickered.

"Oh yeah? Your favorite? What about Tamsyn Muir?" I asked.

They scratched their head and frowned.

"Okay, my other favorite Kiwi author."

Diana chuckled and chided the themby next, asking, "And what about Issy Waldrom?"

Ginger groaned, and her voice dropped to a mumble.

"My other. . . other favorite Kiwi author."

Everyone laughed as the meeting came to a close.

When the room was empty aside from Frankie and myself, I started pushing abandoned chairs in while she raised an eyebrow.

"Old habit," I said, shrugging. "Can't leave a place messier than I found it."

Frankie's tummy then chose that time to make the loudest complaint known to man. I think there were Tibetan monks on the other side of the planet who heard it. She looked torn between wanting to tear her stomach out and dissolving into a puddle of embarrassment that would immediately seek out the nearest floor drain.

"C'mon, Frankie. Let's get you an actual meal. When was the last time you ate before that plate of chips?"

She attempted to shrug and wobbled a little bit as I guided her to the bar.

"Hey Chris, can you get this poor starving girl a burger and fries er — " I paused looking at Frankie. "Veggie burger?"

She shook her head and looked at the floor miserably like she couldn't believe this was happening. Oh, it was happening, alright. But it would be okay because I was nothing, if not, a nurturing soul. Nurturing was fun because you got to poke at people and lightly tease them when they were at their weakest moments.

I never claimed to be nurturing AND kind, I thought, grinning as Chris took the cash I offered.

"I can Venmo you," Frankie said, her stomach making enough noise that the men playing guitar on stage couldn't drown it out.

"No worries," I said, taking another sip of my tea. "Seriously, though, when did you last eat?"

Frankie's eyes nearly rolled back into their sockets. Apparently, asking her to do math on an empty stomach was a violation of the 8th Amendment.

"I think I had a bowl of oatmeal for breakfast," she said.

"You THINK?!" I nearly scolded.

She flinched and stared down at the bar until

Chris brought her food out, which she made vanish faster than the Joker's pencil.

Frankie honest to gods belched as she pushed her plate away, and I couldn't help but burst out laughing.

"You're an interesting gal, Frankie Dee," I said, tracing a finger along the edge of my glass.

She attempted to get her fluster under control and took a long gulp of her second cider. It wasn't working well — the controlling her fluster bit. The cider was working beautifully.

"Sorry about that. Um, so, what do you like to do aside from reading, Dawn?"

She's worked up to small talk. That's certainly an advancement, I thought.

"Well, I like to garden. I sometimes take off up to The County to hunt. And I manage an annual fundraiser for the Merrill Theatre downtown."

"Wow, you stay busy," Frankie said, asking Chris for a third cider.

"Not so busy that I forget to eat. What do you like to do aside from reading and work?"

And, for the first time, I watched Frankie with a little bit of worry in my gut as she rubbed the side of her head, staring at her glass. It looked like she was trying to think of a complex equation, but all I'd asked about were her hobbies. It shouldn't have been a difficult question.

Unless. . . she legitimately doesn't have any, I thought, trying to imagine how hard one would have to work to fill up every single second of the day not involved in sleeping. A tiny pit formed in the bottom of my gut, and I was suddenly overwhelmed by a strange desire to change that for her, which made no sense. This was a complete stranger. I'd known her for all of three hours at this point.

And yet. . . the desire remained, an all-consuming prompt at the base of my skull, and I knew it wasn't going to change. So, picturing the Two of Cups again, I said, "Forget it. Do you want to get out of here?"

Frankie Dee's eyes widened until they were larger than the plate she obliterated her burger and fries on. I watched her fingers twitch and that staring started again.

After a solid 30 seconds, she finally cleared her throat and asked, "Where. . . did you want to go?"

"How about back to my place?" I said.

A tiny squeak escaped from Frankie's lips, and I found myself grinning like the Cheshire cat, suddenly curious about what other noises I might be able to coax from her.

"I — I really shouldn't. I've gotta get home and look over some documents from the city before bed. And early tomorrow morning, I'm meeting our newest editor. Not to mention. . .," her voice trailed off getting lost somewhere, along with her brown eyes in mine. They seemed so vibrant and hungry for something new, and I wanted to give it to her.

My heart was already fluttering a little because

of the way she looked at me. It was like I was some kind of goddess sitting next to her in a brewery full of people who didn't matter and never would. All that mattered was her answer to my question. And it was one she didn't seem to have finished yet.

I egged her on with a raised eyebrow and a slightly turned head.

"Mmmm?" I barely prompted her.

Her hands fumbled with her phone as she quickly turned it off. Not locked the screen. Turned the whole damn device off. Powered down entirely. Nobody was going to reach Frankie except for the witch sitting next to her.

"Fuck it. We ball," she said, finishing her drink, nearly falling off her stool, and closing her tab once she regained her balance.

I paid my own tab, led her out to my Subaru, and thought, *We ball indeed.*

3

(Dawn)

The ride to my Craftsman bungalow in Brighton Corner didn't take but 10 minutes, which wasn't bad from East Bayside. I'd never been able to afford living on the peninsula and after several years of renting in Deering, Woodfords, and the Back Cove, I finally found a house on June Street that was perfect.

From the moment I saw it, I knew the home had everything I wanted, from a gated yard bordering a small patch of woods to a front yard garden just waiting to be nursed back to health through careful attention and love.

"Wow. You've got quite a pretty little house there. I can only imagine what it costs to rent," Frankie said, eyes widening as we pulled into the driveway.

June Street was tucked away on Portland's west side not far from Shay's, one of the less popular food store chains that was doing all it could to survive the onslaught of Grocery Basket and Henneford Supermarket (Hennie's as the locals sometimes called it).

Trees surrounded the entire street. It only had about four houses on it, counting mine.

A great-horned owl hooted in the oak tree that leaned a little closer to my covered porch every year.

"Oh, I don't rent. This pretty little parlor is all mine," I said, beaming. "Well — it's the bank's until I pay it off in 25 years, but semantics."

Frankie turned to me and whistled.

"Owning property in Portland before 30? Who did I go home with tonight? A trust fund child From Away?"

I snickered.

"Partially right. I am From Away. I definitely don't have a trust fund. But how do you know I'm under 30?"

Frankie Dee shrugged and got out of my car.

"I dunno, bub. Just always been good at guessing ages. You still seem like you're a couple of years away from that threshold."

Walking around the vehicle and leaning on its hood, I crossed my arms and raised an eyebrow.

"Flatterer. Save your compliments. I already took you home, didn't I? And don't tell me you're one of those women who think life is all downhill once your age no longer starts with a two."

I saw Frankie eyeing my garden full of sprouted daffodils, perky and defiant of any remaining April snow or chill. I loved that about those stubborn little flowers.

For a moment, Frankie bore a more melancholic expression as she stared at nothing in particular.

"Ha. No, life isn't all downhill after 30. Age doesn't mean much to me. In my eyes, there's just work that needs to be done. Whether you're 20 or 60, the work ain't going anywhere."

Holy hell, who killed this woman's spirit? I thought, elbowing my new friend in the ribs, which elicited a small stammer of surprise and was quickly followed by a breathless giggle.

"Go back to complimenting my house," I said. "I've put a lot of work into it."

Frankie Dee snorted and looked over at the two-story home I'd pumped more blood, sweat, and cash into than I cared to admit. It was still an almost 70-year-old home, but the fresh grey paint I added last fall still looked pretty damn good.

"I like how your window frames are red to match the front door," Frankie said, taking time to look over my house. "And the little stone steps painted like flowers leading up to the front door are cute. This place just seems so. . . whole, ya know? Carefully put together piece by piece."

Well, shit. I'd jokingly told her to compliment my home, and she'd done just that. Only her words had gone past inspiring pride and instead left even me a little emotionally hamstrung as I fought a growing blush.

Still, a part of me enjoyed the attention on a place I'd worked for years to fix up. A human being was here right in front of me appreciating something I'd busted my ass to make nice. Month after month of YouTube tutorials, trips to House Depot, and weekend warrior projects that almost left me feeling a little too white picket fence at times.

And Frankie's praise wasn't like internet comments that felt good for a few minutes but then vanished like cotton candy accidentally dropped into a puddle. They were warm words being said to my face, by a really cute girl that I wanted to bring inside and kiss.

Instead of doing that, I found myself asking, "You want to see the back? I'll show you my kid."

Frankie Dee just stood there blinking.

"You have a kid?"

I nodded, grinning mischievously and pointing with my chin. We walked over to a gate on the side of my house as motion lights kicked on, bathing us in pale beams. A six-foot wooden privacy fence surrounded my backyard on the sides. It transitioned to ranch fencing and chicken wire on the side facing the woods.

My backyard wasn't huge by any means. A small chicken coop I'd built from scrap wood a neighbor gladly gave me sat close to the house. I bruised my thumbs so much that weekend that I had trouble moving them for days afterward. And the curses I hissed that day probably killed at least a rose bush or two elsewhere in the neighborhood.

Frankie followed me as more motion lights kicked on, and a small bleating sound echoed from the back porch. That's when she came into view, half running/half hobbling in the way my kid often did.

A black and white pygmy goat that didn't even come up to my knees bleated happily and bumped her head into my leg. She was entirely snow-colored except for splotches of black on her front legs and over her eyes.

"Frankie Dee, I want you to meet Billie," I said, picking up the 17-pound goat.

This was her true test. I watched for signs of disgust or flinching, but in two seconds Frankie's face went from curious about the noise to full-on adoration of my fluffy child.

"Oh my goodness! She's just a little guy!" she cooed and came over to pet her.

Billie wasn't shy. She sniffed and lightly nibbled on Frankie's fingers with her lips. She only had back teeth, so it was actually difficult for her to bite you unless you stuck your fingers in her mouth like a moron.

Frankie oo'ed and aw'ed over my goat for another couple of minutes before she looked up at me with a sneer.

"Wait. . . Billie? As in, Billie the Kid?"

The grin that snuck over my lips was nothing less than pure goofball. And Frankie Dee loved every bit of it. I could tell by the way she shook her head looking at the ground.

"Come on. I'll introduce you to the Fates," I said, setting Billie down and walking my guest over to the chicken coop.

She followed as I opened the latch and slowly unveiled three Buff Orpington hens who clucked a little but otherwise remained on their nests of straw and pine shavings, staring at us. Most of their feathers were a light gold color with their necks taking on more of a brownish hue. Their combs were as red as my front door.

"Hey there, ladies. Don't mind me. Just showing you off to my new friend," I said, letting Frankie peek in for a closer look.

"Oh wow! You've got some stout ladies in there," she giggled. "Fresh eggs?"

I nodded.

"That, and they help control ticks and snakes in the backyard."

My new friend turned to me and managed to fight her fluster just long enough to ask, "So, if I stay the night, does that mean I get scrambled eggs in the morning?"

I raised an eyebrow and asked, "Are you staying the night?"

She shook her head.

"With a stranger? Sorry, no. I don't care how pretty she is. I'm not staying the night with someone I've known for less time than it'd take me to watch 'Return of the King.'"

Leaning against the chicken coop, I batted my eyelashes at Frankie and said with the sweetest voice I could muster, "But what if I put on 'Return of the King?' Would you stay the night then?" It was almost cartoonish the way I asked with a leering smirk.

"Theatrical edition?" Frankie asked, sounding entirely serious.

"Yeah," I replied.

"No."

I frowned.

"Extended edition?" she asked, again appearing deliberate.

"Sure."

"Still no," Frankie said, laughing.

I shook my head and led the newest book club member inside my house after petting Billie some more.

My living room is wide open and consists mostly of a corner sofa and a small television perched on an antique chest I thought looked rustic.

A blue and white rug stretched out from under my couch for several feet before it surrendered to a hardwood floor.

In the corner, a petrified tree stump sat on a thin

black rug. It was covered in purple and silver candles that surrounded a tiny, hand-sized cauldron filled with tiny bones, smoky quartz, and crow feathers. The cauldron rested on a wooden case containing my Wise Goat Tarot cards. An incense holder carved in the shape of a raven sat on the very back of the stump.

The shrine immediately drew Frankie Dee's stare, and I greeted my visitor with her second test of the night, watching her eyes for immediate disapproval. But I was greeted more with curiosity than anything as she turned to me.

"My shrine to The Morrigan," I said, shrugging.

"Who is that?" Frankie asked.

"Celtic goddess of war and destiny," I said. "I work with her most frequently."

Frankie nodded slowly, looking back at the altar as she rubbed her chin. I couldn't quite read her expression.

"You're, what, Wiccan?" she asked.

I scrunched my face and shook my head.

"I prefer to just call myself a witch or a practicing pagan if you want a term that's a little less Halloween-ish," I said, shrugging again.

Frankie Dee's mouth was a straight line for a moment before she muttered, "fascinating," in a pretty damn good Hank McCoy impression. Though, I doubt that was her intent.

Walking over to the altar, I picked up one of the

feathers from the cauldron and turned to face my new friend.

"I learned most of my starting craft practices from my grandmother. It drove my father mad," I said fighting a flinch at imagining his voice. "But he can fuck off. I loved every moment I had with her and think about her each day I light these candles."

My heart stirred anytime I got to talk about the craft. It felt like the right kind of defiance, and that pride swelled with each episode of Dawn's Divinations I recorded in the morning. My guest grew quiet as I talked.

And soon, I'd have a column in the Portland Lighthouse-Journal, reaching a whole new audience of readers who will hopefully start asking bigger questions with their lives. My meeting with the paper's publisher and managing editor tomorrow to sign the contract was the most important thing on my calendar this month.

Frankie took a step closer to my altar and smiled, putting a hand on my shoulder.

"You're all fired up and passionate. Kind of adds a sexy new layer to the lady who took me home tonight," she said with the full confidence of someone fully expecting to be kissed. I have no clue where she pulled it from, but it did things to me as I leaned closer.

"Gotta say. You're talking an awful lot of game for someone within smooching range," I said.

Her eyes widened, and I watched the deer in the

headlights look overtake a woman who'd only just managed to get a single flirtation out before receiving returning fire. Fuck, Frankie swerved between the lanes of "flirt" and "freeze" like a crazed driver, and all I wanted to do was throw her on the couch and climb on top of this pretty blonde trapped in the full frenzy of gay panic.

With surprising strength, I watched Frankie Dee move her lips closer to mine. It was daring and a bold play for someone who I could paralyze with a stray smile. And yet, I got the feeling she wasn't always like that. I sensed an audacious flavor of strength in this woman. She could waltz into any boardroom or public meeting and say things I'd have to practice for a week to not lose my nerve over.

It's just pretty girls that do her in, I thought, taking a moment to appreciate the warmth and desire radiating from Frankie's lips.

I closed my eyes and finally united our lips like I'd been wanting to since I first laid eyes on our newest book club member at the bar.

Trying not to sound cliche, I quickly realized Frankie was wearing cherry chapstick. And she was so soft and ready for me. The way she seemed to drink me in, the way she pressed her body against mine, and the way she moaned when I took her bottom lip between my teeth, all let me know it'd been a long time since anyone had done this to her. Was no one interested in this incredibly cute girl, or had she simply been too busy to allow someone to treasure her?

Frankie Dee didn't hesitate to let me take control of the kiss and set a tempo. The truth was, she seemed so grateful to have my lips on hers that I doubted she'd object to much in this moment.

I deepened the kiss and moved us over to the couch where Frankie let me lay her down and climb on top while she cupped my face in her hands. Warmth built in my core as she ran her fingers through my hair, found where I'd tied the bandana, undid it and then tossed the thin fabric aside so she could rub the back of my head and neck more freely.

All of that elicited a moan from yours truly, and Frankie's body started to hum like the neon sign of a 24/7 diner.

Running her fingers over my ass and squeezing it, I felt a shiver ride halfway up my spine.

"If you want to do things like that, we'd best move this to the bedroom," I hissed as Frankie Dee started to kiss my neck, and moisture built in the other place I wanted her lips to be.

"Uh. . . huh," she managed in between kisses when we fought for air.

We stumbled through the dim hallway, Frankie's shoulder bumping the wall and threatening to knock over a photo of the sunrise on Casco Bay.

And then, we were on my queen bed, spread out over a red and black duvet. I looked into the hungry brown eyes of my partner for the night and found myself smiling, butterflies doing somersaults in my tummy. She didn't even take a breath before pulling me down to nibble on my collarbone. In response, I moaned and pushed my pelvis into hers for harder contact, cursing the pants on Frankie that kept me from feeling her through the fabric.

Loud bleating from outside brought me back to reality as I sat up and cursed.

"I'm so sorry. I think I forgot to lock up the chicken coop," I said.

Catching her breath and coming down from the heat we were building, Frankie Dee almost groaned in protest as I got up from the bed.

"I'll be right back," I said. "How about, to make up for the momentary disruption, I'll walk back into the room sans dress?"

The blonde woman in my bed honest-to-gods snapped her teeth in my direction, and I found myself lit with fire anew.

Turning to go, I looked back over my shoulder for just a moment.

"Oh, I had your consent to do the thing we were about to do, right? Just wanted to make sure."

With her eyes suddenly drooping, Frankie nodded. And then she yawned, which caused me to turn back around and cross my arms.

"Well, I'm sorry you found our activities so dull, Frankie," I said, grinning and leaning against the door frame.

She rubbed her eyes and then shook her head in a desperate bid not to look exhausted.

"I'm sorry. I was at the office at 4 a.m. this morning for an interview, and your bed is fucking comfy. But I'll be SO ready when you get back," Frankie said.

Holy shit. Who arrives at the office that early? I thought, fighting a frown. It's already midnight, and she came straight from work at 7 tonight.

Pushing those thoughts aside, I ran outside to close the chicken coop, made sure Billie's water was full and accessible, and came back in.

Taking a deep breath in the hallway, I stripped to my black bra and panties, sauntering back into the bedroom, trying hard not to leap on Frankie and immediately resume our rather explicit activities.

"Now. . . where were we?" I asked in a saucy voice that took years of practice to get just right.

When I didn't get an immediate response, I thought, *Damn. She's frozen in awe at the sight of me. No doubt about it, Dawn. You've still got it.*

Light snoring immediately shattered my thoughts as I looked more closely at the bed to find my partner. . . entirely passed out.

Motherfucker! I thought. *I either really did bore her, or she truly was exhausted after working a 14-hour shift.*

Scanning the bags under her eyes, I sighed.

"For the sake of my ego, I'm going to assume it's the latter," I muttered, finding a fuzzy white blanket I stole from an ex named Brittany, and covering my date for the night. My incredibly cute and incredibly frustrating date.

Changing into my comfy pajamas and turning out the lights, I decided to bunk on the couch tonight. It took a while to fall asleep as all my effort went into not thinking about what we'd been doing on this very couch just minutes ago.

4

(Frankie)

The sound of a bleating goat and clucking hens outside slowly drew my mind back toward consciousness. And this alarmed me for two reasons.

First: I didn't have goats or chickens.

Second: Neither of those noises was the sound I selected for my 4:30 a.m. alarm.

I tried to jolt awake, but my body seemed to be in lazy mode, limbs moving in slow motion and rebelling against me. This was a more common occurrence of late with the longer shifts I'd been working. Should that have worried me? Perhaps. But I had a newspaper to save. If my body didn't want to cooperate, I'd just have to push it that much harder.

Stretching and yawning, I found myself tucked in with a white fuzzy blanket.

The fuck? I thought, seconds before it all came

rushing back to me. I'd gone home with a member of my book club after an ill-advised third cider. Somewhere in the back of my mind, I heard myself say the words "fuck it, we ball." And that should have been a sign I was out of my goddamn mind.

The pretty brunette drove me. . . here, wherever here was. Brighton Corner?

"Did we fuck?" I asked myself, puzzled, trying to recall the previous night. I remembered making out on her couch. I remembered Billie the Kid and the Fates in her backyard. And then. . . it all went black.

Looking under the blanket, I confirmed my clothes were still on and quite wrinkled by now. Fumbling around for my phone, I found it plugged in next to me on the nightstand, and the time — well, that couldn't be right! The time said 9:27 a.m. And I had several missed texts and calls.

I overslept! I thought, bolting out of the bed and looking around for my mysteriously witchy date from the previous night. She was nowhere to be found.

Her room was gorgeous in a macabre sort of way, with walls painted a dark shade of purple and a few beaded posters of what appeared to be goddesses hanging here and there.

A long oak dresser sat opposite the bed with another altar on top. Curious, I walked over and found several twigs and a book of pressed leaves and flowers. Two carvings of deer sat across from each other on opposite sides of the altar with a few vials of what I desperately hoped was animal blood tied to a bundle of sticks. A small silver basin with a bowstring inside stood closest to the altar's edge.

"I wonder if this is also for The Morrigan," I muttered, getting my face a little closer to the altar than I should have.

After checking to make sure I had both my kidneys and no punctures on my neck, I giggled and walked out into the hallway to find a bathroom. A fresh towel, packaged toothbrush, hairbrush, and a whole pantsuit sat waiting, presumably for me.

"How the fuck. . . did I go home with an Airbnb host last night?" I asked. "Am I supposed to wear. . . her clothes?"

Checking my phone again, I flinched and hopped into the shower without a second thought. I didn't have any time to stop by my home this morning.

The pantsuit was a little loose on me, but I didn't care. I rushed into the kitchen, hoping to find my witchy date and ask her for a ride to work. Before I could get the question out, my stomach grumbled with all the noise of a bellowing hippo.

And I smelled. . . coffee? Bacon?

Sitting in the coffeemaker was a warm pot of dark roast. Bacon and scrambled eggs sat in a warm skillet on the stove with a glass lid on. Lifting the lid and letting the steam out, my stomach nearly tore out of my body like a xenomorph to dive into that pile of eggs.

"She remembered my comment about the eggs," I mumbled, feeling warmth seep into my chest.

"Dawn? Are you here?" I called to an empty house.

A plate, fork, mug, and cloth napkin had already been set out for me.

I ate at the bar in her kitchen, finding a wooden stool to sit on tucked into a corner. Looking around at the hanging herbs and antique cabinets, I found myself wondering about the girl I went home with last night and where she was now.

As if on cue, I spotted a small note on the bar with extra loopy handwriting.

It read, "Frankie, as requested, please enjoy a skillet of scrambled eggs. You quickly fell asleep last night, and I am nothing if not a good hostess. Sorry to leave so early, but I have a business meeting of sorts in town at 10:30 a.m. and a few errands to take care of before that. I hope the pantsuit fits. An ex-girlfriend left it here, and I just never got around to donating the clothes. I guess Fate wanted you to have it. Feel free to keep the outfit as I don't need it. Have a great day! - Dawn."

My cheeks heated as I re-read the note twice to make sure I understood. I'd fallen asleep. We were going to have sex, and I. . . fucking fell asleep. Oh my god, this could not be more mortifying.

Several months without sex, and despite fucking every-thing up last night, I, myself, remained thoroughly un-fucked, I thought.

I pressed my face into my hands and groaned. In a way, it was actually a small mercy Dawn had left me alone. I wasn't sure I had the guts to face her again after last night.

Embarrassment raked its claws across my chest, and I felt every bit a fool. My first fling since Margaret dumped me, and I fell asleep before I could be flung. The only thing more embarrassing would have been puking on Dawn. But I was no Stevie Scott. However, the woman who took me home last night had a few Iris Kelly qualities.

"Well, shit," I muttered, taking a bite of the fluffiest scrambled eggs I'd ever eaten in my life. Hot damn. Backyard chickens were a gift after all.

I devoured breakfast, washed my dishes (because if Dawn was a good hostess, then I was damn sure going to be a good guest), made the bed, and went outside to hop into an Uber.

In the light, Dawn's home looked even more adorable, almost like the trees around it were shielding the house from any threats that might come its way. And I wouldn't be surprised if that was literally the case since I apparently almost fucked a witch.

A calendar notification on my phone reminded me I had my own fortune teller to meet with at the newspaper so we could hire our new horoscope editor. Glancing back at the house one more time, I muttered, "Goodbye, Dawn. Sorry to ruin your night, but good news, you'll never see me again."

I made a solemn vow to quit the book club right then and there. What was I thinking? I didn't have time for an extra meeting every month. And now I'd be reminded of ruining a perfectly -good evening with the prettiest girl in the group at every event I attended.

Looking at my online bookstore cart, I debated whether I wanted to cancel my order of *The Tea Dragon Tapestry*.

Scratching my head, I thought, *It does look really cute. Maybe I can just keep it and read the graphic novel on my own time.*

I WALKED into the newsroom a little after 10 a.m. and was met with a few stares and quiet coughs. Behind me, Emma was the first one to speak, and that was her first mistake of the day.

"Wow, first you leave early and then arrive late. Who are you, and what have you done with our managing editor?"

"Radio Girl, I swear to God, I will demote you to unpaid intern if you don't shut the fuck up," I said, turning to my snickering evening editor. "Also, why are you here?"

She pointed toward the conference room with her chin.

"I wanted to attend the morning news meeting to pitch a new series on historic homes in the city," she said.

I raised an eyebrow.

"And how did that pitch go?"

"Mr. Ricci approved it. I'll start writing up the first piece tonight."

I rolled my eyes.

"That's because my father is a fucking softie, bub. You get three, and they will run in the Monday edition at the back of Section D," I said, narrowing my eyes.

"You got it," Emma said, turning to leave.

I rubbed my forehead, trying not to overreact at the fact that I missed my first morning news meeting in seven years. Even if I was out of town or sick, I'd always call in. As my blood pressure spiked, I took a deep breath and worked on clearing my inbox until it was time to meet with the woman I hoped would be our new Horoscope Editor.

My father leaned into the office.

"Morning," he said.

I looked up and wiped my forehead again.

"Good morning. Thanks for running the news meeting. I'm sorry I was late."

My father used to be a much bigger man. He clocked in at just under 300 pounds before his heart attack. But he'd been doing better since then and slimmed down quite a bit. His last doctor visit saw him down to 249. All things considered, I was proud of him.

He was a shorter man who somehow kept a full head of curly blond hair. My father wore a thin goatee and a white button-down shirt with a pair of pressed jeans. His brown eyes sat atop a nest of wrinkles from years of service to our family newspaper. Left before sunup, home after sunset.

Broad shoulders and a sterner face than his actual personality left others under the impression Mr. Ricci was a steamroller. The truth was, our publisher was a big softie. He let his appearance take the place of verbal muscle when running the newsroom, and the Lighthouse-Journal prospered all the more for it until his trip to the ER.

"I wasn't worried. A girl barely in her 30s missing a single meeting? Well, it was almost a relief. You've been pushing yourself so hard lately. I was worried you'd snap," he said, stepping closer and patting me on the shoulder. "I'm glad you took the morning to sleep in, grab an actual breakfast, and maybe even pray a little for our paper, huh?"

My father smiled, and I smiled soon after. It was our way of telling each other everything was alright. His grin came easily. And when Mr. Ricci started, I couldn't help but return the expression. He was my Dad, and all I ever wanted to be was like him. From the age of four, I was helping him run evening news meetings after preschool.

He bought me a little stool, and I proudly stood on top and wrote gibberish on the chalkboard as reporters and editors pitched their stories. Whenever the meeting slowed down a little, he'd glance up at me and ask, "You get that, FeeDee?"

I would nod with a serious expression and prepare to write down the next story pitch.

"You think God is going to save our newspaper, Dad?"

"Well, it can't hurt to ask, huh?"

Another grin. My father, ever the faithful Catholic. Publicly, he credited the doctors at Maine Medical Hospital for saving his life during a heart attack. Privately, he gave thanks to God. I didn't care who got credit. I was just happy to have my dad safe.

"You don't think God will smite our paper for introducing a horoscope section?" I asked, standing up.

He put an arm around my shoulder as we walked out of the office and over toward the conference room.

"Naaahhhhh," my father said, waving a hand. "It's just entertainment. Like movies or the Facebook. Just for shits and giggles."

"Oh, like baseball?" I asked with a coy smile.

He stopped and took his arm from around my shoulder. Now I'd done it.

"Young lady, some things in this life are too sacred to blasphemy. And America's favorite pastime is one of them! For the sake of the Blue Sox and Saint Anthony Ramera on third base, I command thee to repent," he nearly shouted.

It was difficult to get my father angry. But you didn't fuck with his baseball. Once in a while, though, I couldn't resist.

From the features desk, I heard Isabelle holler, "Young lady, if you say that shit again, I'm gonna have to confess to Father Carlos what I did to you."

I turned to her and crossed my arms.

"You're aware that I'm your boss, right?"

"You're aware that the Blue Sox were the 2022 World Series champions, right?"

Rolling my eyes and walking toward the conference room with my muttering father in tow, I rounded the corner to find my second shock of the day.

Sitting at the end of our circular meeting table behind a paper Moonbucks coffee cup was none other than Dawn Summers.

My heart came to a screeching halt, and Franky Jr. nearly collided with me since I stopped right in the doorway, more frozen than the world's smuggest smuggler in carbonite.

If the witch looked surprised to see me, she hid it well. However, Dawn did raise an eyebrow and placed her chin on her fist.

"Dawn!" I gasped, much worse at controlling my outbursts in the presence of a beautiful woman.

She sat there in a cheap, outdated, and certainly

uncomfortable wooden chair wearing a blue blouse and a white skirt with matching tights underneath. Her lips were painted a soft pink, and a tiny mouse skull on a leather cord sat nestled around Dawn's neck.

"Frankie," she replied with a near chuckle, her green eyes wide with amusement.

I'm starting to suspect this woman knows what she does to me, I thought, fighting and losing a war with my warming cheeks. I watched the witch adjust the headband holding her brown curls in place.

Thus far, my plan to never see Dawn again was off to a shitty start.

"Thank you for coming in, Ms. Summers," my father said, extending a hand and ignoring his stammering idiot of a daughter. "I'm really looking forward to what you'll do with our new astrology section. I don't know shit about star signs, but I trust you'll keep it interesting."

Dawn shook his hand and offered a beaming smile that pierced my chest like an arrow fired from Robin Hood's bow.

There were two things I needed at this very moment: her lips on my body and a time machine so I could go back and stop that witch from putting her lips on my body. While these desires warred within me, Franky Jr. sat at the table and looked up at me.

"What's the matter, FeeDee?"

Dawn stifled a huge laugh and covered it with a

cough. I could practically hear her shouting, "FeeDee?!"

I scowled at the witch, cursed my luck, and shook my head.

"No, Dad. Um, everything's fine."

His face scrunched as the publisher looked back and forth between the two of us, and I prayed to the good Lord in Heaven that I be raptured immediately to save me from this meeting. How could I not remember the girl I'd been emailing was also named Dawn Summers?!

"Do you two know each other?" he asked.

It took everything I had to keep from running out of the room screaming. Do we know each other? Almost Biblically, father. My hands started to rise toward my face to hide my expression, but I forced them back down to my sides.

"Why, yes, Mr. Ricci. Your daughter and I met at a book club last night," Dawn said.

He looked over at me.

"You met Dawn at a book club last night, and you didn't know she was the Horoscope Editor we're about to hire?" Franky Jr. asked, not upset, just confused. His daughter could write 800 words of copy on new tax law and state budgetary procedure without missing a single fact, but throw a pretty girl into the mix, and she was fucked.

Well, almost fucked, I thought. *If I hadn't fallen asleep!*

Turning to my dad, I forced a small nod.

"I guess it just. . . didn't occur to me," I said.

Dawn spoke up.

"Don't worry. She was probably just tired last night. Frankie spent half the meeting looking like she was about to. . . I dunno. . . fall asleep or something."

When my father looked back at our witchy guest, I threw her the most dirty and scathing scowl I could muster. The edges of her lips curled in response. I could almost mentally picture her giving me a dainty wave and blowing me a kiss in mockery.

This can't be happening! I thought, unsure of whether I wanted to snap at her or ask her to grab the back of my neck and kiss me with last night's force again.

The publisher cleared his throat, and I finally sat down next to him.

"Well, you've had a chance to look over the contract, yes? You'll come aboard as our new Horoscope Editor for three months, and we'll reevaluate how our readers respond at the end of that quarter. How's that sound?"

Dawn nodded at him and locked eyes with me again before saying, "Oh, I'm very much looking forward to starting work here."

(Frankie)

———————————————————

Dawn left before I got a chance to talk to her after the contract signing, and it grated on my nerves leaving unfinished business in the air. I couldn't text her because I didn't have her number. Could I show up at her house unannounced? Perhaps. Did I want to be a creeper AND a failed one-night stand? Not a chance.

So, the only option left was to wait until today. I'd gotten up at 4:30 a.m. like usual, lamented the lack of scrambled eggs in my home, swallowed some awful instant coffee, and got to the newsroom.

Living on Munjoy Hill meant work was just a five-minute walk away, and I loved that about our office's location.

Sitting at my computer, I started proofreading the first draft of an editorial we were publishing this weekend on an upcoming election that could limit how many cruise ships were allowed to visit Portland each year.

"The DSA sure is proactive. I'll give them that," I muttered, ignoring my groaning stomach.

Just let me finish this, and I'll grab something from the vending machine, I thought, patting my tummy.

I broke that promise and many others I made to myself as the morning wore on. There was just too much to look through. I barely even got five seconds to stand up from my desk in between looking through the city's response to my FOIA request and taking a phone call from an alderman upset about our coverage on a vote over an affordable housing development in Bayside.

My stomach had all but given up growling, and my body had moved on to being slightly dizzy when Craig stepped into my office. He stood around six feet tall with almond eyes and pale skin. He was freshly graduated from the Maine University South and eager to cut his teeth on anything and everything we could throw at him.

The boy's curly, bouncy black hair and radiant golden retriever energy were almost too much on some days, especially mornings when I'd neglected breakfast. Today he wore a red cardigan and slacks, along with freshly-polished shoes.

"Morning, Boss!"

"Don't call me that," I said, leaning forward over my desk. "Watcha need, Craig?"

He cleared his throat and checked his phone.

"I had a story I wanted to pitch."

I looked up and raised an eyebrow.

"Your pitch can't wait for the morning meeting?" I asked.

Craig shifted his legs, clearly still not used to feeling strain or pushback from a manager or editor. I don't know how they let kids out of the journalism program at MUS without toughening them up a bit.

You don't get to be an inky wretch by squirming under pressure, I thought. *He's got great potential. Kid's just gotta toughen up a little.*

To that end, I'd been a little more stern with him these last few months, trying to get him to grow some legs to stand on. The results thus far were. . . mixed.

"Well, it's just, if I'm going to do this story, I need to get the interview done today. And the interviewee needs to know in the next hour for scheduling purposes."

I stifled a sigh. This sounded like last-second planning, and I wasn't too keen on it. Then again, Craig was our general assignment reporter. We threw him at everything that needed coverage, breaking news, city meetings, new museum exhibits, court cases, and more. It's the best position for fresh college grads because they can run their wheels in a bunch of different directions and figure out what beats to specialize in. If he had a good story idea, I wasn't opposed to giving him a chance to seize it, provided he could make a solid case for coverage.

"Okay, Craig. Tell me about your story."

His eyes lit up, and I watched his unsure posture melt away like butter in a warm pan.

"There's this Australian DJ performing at the Statehouse Theatre tomorrow night. Her name is Demon Grrl. And she lands at the Jetport in a couple of hours, where I can run over and interview her if you approve my story."

I rested my chin on my palm while I listened.

"What makes this DJ newsworthy?"

Craig cleared his throat again, and I waited patiently while he tried to work out the exact wording of his justification.

"Well, she's trans. And she's kicking off a US tour where half of all her concert proceeds will be donated to The Tyler Project, which works to prevent suicide in queer youth and adults. I think there's an interesting piece to be written on why this issue was so important to her that she traveled halfway around the world to raise money for it. And it's timely given recent bills here in Maine that bolstered trans-gender medical protections while bills in New Hampshire were aimed at restricting trans rights."

I had initially thought Craig was pitching me a puff piece, but the way he'd tied the article into timely political news in the region impressed me. I nodded and stood from my desk. Maybe the kid was growing a bit after all.

With a soft smile, I said, "Okay, I'm sold. Run out to the Jetport and interview your DJ. But! This isn't just a musical profile piece. You have to get the Aussie to talk about why this tour is so important to her and ask about Maine's recent trans protection legislation you mentioned. Maybe even ask her to compare the current U.S. political climate for trans issues to what things are like where she lives."

The golden retriever standing in my office returned my smile with a wide grin and nodded eagerly. The kid understood his assignment perfectly. And I had no doubt he'd turn in an excellent piece. His writing wasn't the issue. It was his confidence that needed work. Hopefully, this would help a little with that.

"How'd this Demon Grrl even get on your radar?" I asked.

Craig scratched the back of his head.

"Well, my little brother is trans, and he listens to her music a lot when he's playing Minecraft. I can hardly visit home without hearing one of her songs playing from the speakers in his room. He's even tweeted her a few times, and she responded. She has all these songs about cyborgs and identity. It's pretty neat."

I tried to remember if Craig had mentioned having a queer sibling before, but nothing came to mind, so I just nodded.

"She's gotten really popular over the last few years. I watched a few clips of her competing on the Australian version of *The X Factor*. Demon Grrl made it to one of the last rounds before being eliminated."

Behind Craig, I saw a certain witch walk into the newsroom, and my attention quickly shifted. But before I got hypnotized by Dawn's wandering green eyes, I shook my head and turned back to the young reporter.

"Well, that all sounds good. Off to the Jetport with ya, bub. Keep the article under 40 inches, and we'll run it in tomorrow's culture section."

"You got it, Boss."

The kid gave me a mock salute and turned to leave, typing something on his phone, probably texting the DJ.

I'll work on getting him to ditch the salute after he stops calling me 'Boss', I thought, rolling my eyes.

After Craig left, I was tempted to run out and — what? Pull Dawn aside to kiss her? No! Stop it, brain. We rehearsed this before bed last night. We're going to have a calm conversation about our professional relationship and nothing more.

I took a deep breath.

And it'll look desperate if I rush over to her and start talking about our previous. . . encounter, I thought.

So I used all my self-control to just casually wave at Dawn as our eyes met. Just a simple greeting and she'd calmly walk to her desk and

— oh shit — oh fuck. She's coming over here. Was that a "come over here" wave? I could have sworn it was a "Nice to see you. Please stay over there" wave.

My blood pressure might have spiked. Maybe the floor wiggled a bit. I couldn't be sure. Regularly skipping breakfast will do that to a girl.

"Morning, Frankie," Dawn said.

"Dawn," I nodded, unsure of how to proceed. Fortunately, the witch didn't seem to have any trouble finding a segway into our next words.

"You look a little pale," she said.

I shook my head.

"Excuse me?"

"You skipped breakfast again, didn't you?"

"H — how did you know?"

Dawn grinned and held up a paper bag I hadn't noticed in her hand. Was I so distracted by her black sheath dress that I failed to realize she was carrying the sack? If I kept this up, she was *definitely* going to know what she did to my poor heart.

"Because you weren't this pale yesterday when you devoured the eggs and bacon I left out for you. Thanks for doing the dishes, by the way," she said in a voice that was just a little too loud for my liking.

Quickly ushering her into my office and closing the door, I watched her take out some napkins, a few flakey biscuits, and a small jar of strawberry jam.

"What are you doing?" I asked.

"Making sure my new coworker doesn't pass out by providing freshly baked biscuits and homemade jam?" she said.

I was about to say something stupid when my stomach thankfully interrupted with the song of its people. Endangered right whales in the Gulf of Maine probably heard me from here.

"If you want, I can play the part of a worried housewife who realizes you forgot your lunch and drove to the office to bring it to you," Dawn said, practically thrusting a jam-covered biscuit into my hands. "Who knows? Maybe a little role-play will help keep you awake this time?"

That last line sent a shiver down my spine, and I nearly dropped the biscuit, just barely catching it between my bumbling hands. The witch just smiled.

Well, shit. Dawn knows EXACTLY what she's doing to me, I thought, glumly.

Taking a deep breath and putting the food on my desk, I wiped my fingers with one of the witch's napkins.

"Okay, Dawn. That's exactly what I need to talk to you about."

"Role-play?"

"Yes — I mean no!" I stammered while she giggled. "I'm sorry I really messed up the other night between us. It was embarrassing, and I don't have a clue why it happened."

Dawn raised an eyebrow and actually frowned a little.

"Really? It's a mystery to you? You can pen a column on the effects of property tax increases, but you can't see that you're overworking yourself?"

Everything came to a complete stop for me as I paused and softened my voice.

"You read my column this morning?"

"What do you think I was doing while I waited for the biscuits to bake? I was reading the paper, silly."

I don't know why that moved me so much. But my blood pressure wasn't spiking anymore. Instead, I was left with this strange warm feeling of appreciation. Was it hot in here? Or was I just caught off guard by the fact that the most beautiful lady in all of Maine confessed to reading my column in the paper? That just made me want to kiss her all the more.

Leaning a little closer, I noticed Dawn didn't even flinch. The witch stood exactly where she had been, waiting for me to — no! Stop it, brain. We've got work to do, boundaries to set!

Coughing, I stuffed my face with a biscuit to buy some time while I tried to remember the words I practiced saying in the mirror last night. Okay, boundaries. You can do this, Frankie Dee. You're the managing editor of Maine's largest newspaper. Let's get it done.

"Good stuff," I mumbled, crumbs falling from my mouth.

"I couldn't agree more," Dawn said, watching me with nothing less than a full smile on her face.

When I finally finished the biscuit, Dawn inexplicably handed me a Moonbucks tea she produced. Was that in her other hand the entire time?! My attention to detail outside of the written word drastically needed an overhaul.

Taking a drink of hibiscus tea. I cleared my throat.

"Thank you, Dawn. I really appreciate. . . all this. But I need to be completely honest with you."

"All ears," the witch said.

"Good. I didn't expect to find you in the office the morning after we went home together. Er — to your home, I mean. Judging by your expression yesterday, I don't think you expected me to be the one offering you a contract to become our new Horoscope Editor. But here we are. You signed it. I signed it. And now we're business partners."

Dawn ate a biscuit and nodded.

"That seems like a pretty good summary of yesterday's events," she said, not bored, just patiently waiting for me to get to the point. I guess all those words I'd spewed were an onramp of sorts.

"Right. Yes. Good. Um, as business partners, I don't think we should. . . fraternize. I think you're amazing. I don't regret going home with you. But I think from this point on, we should keep things p— professional," I stuttered, saying words I wasn't entirely sure matched how I felt about Dawn inside.

And if I expected her to throw a fit, or at the very least, sneer, I was shocked. She just nodded, ate another biscuit, and said, "Sure thing. . . FeeDee."

I choked on my tea and gasped for air.

"You will NOT call me that! Or I will shred your fucking contract and scatter the pieces in the sea," I snapped, scowling at the witch who seemed immune.

She waved off my consternation.

"Fine, fine. So we can't date because of work. How about this, instead? You spend some time with me learning about witchcraft to familiarize yourself with what I'll be adding to the Lighthouse-Journal. And I'll spend some time with you learning about journalism to familiarize myself with the publication I'll be bringing my magic to."

Rubbing the bridge of my nose, I stifled a yawn.

"Yeah, sure. That sounds like fun. But we keep it professional, yeah?"

Dawn shrugged.

"Sure. We'll keep the fondling to a minimum."

I scowled, suddenly remembering what she did with her hands as we made out on her couch and trying to fight another shiver surfing down my spine.

Dawn slowly sipped her own tea.

I sidestepped her boundary test and thought for a moment.

"Can I ask a witchcraft question now?"

She nodded.

"Why do you have two shrines to The Morrigan? The design of each seems pretty different."

Dawn's eyes suddenly lit up in a way I'd only seen Craig replicate so far today. And she put down her tea.

"Oh, you mean the bedroom shrine? That one's for Artemis."

"You worship two goddesses?" I asked.

She made a wheel motion with her hand and slowly shook her head from side to side like I hadn't quite used the right words.

"Not really worship. More like. . . I work with them. They guide me. Show me wisdom. Teach me to see what others miss. In exchange, I honor them with altars and leave them regular offerings. It's not a traditional worship like you'd see in a Christian church," she said before raising an eyebrow. "Is that where you find yourself on Sunday mornings?"

I grinned. Guilty.

"Well, don't tell Father Carlos, but I'm only in a pew once a month or so when work allows."

"Catholic?"

"Yes, but not overwhelmingly so. I like the music. I like some of the teachings. But a lot of the dogma is overbearing, so I tune it out."

Dawn cocked her head to the side with neither a frown nor a grin.

"So, working with a witch isn't going to be an issue for you?" she asked.

I scoffed.

"Until this last round of voluntary buyouts, our cops and courts reporter was a card-carrying Satanist. I don't give a shit about personal beliefs. As long as you're not a cannibal or a Jared Leto fan, we've got no issues," I said.

With a growing smile, Dawn asked, "So. . . Catholic, but not overwhelmingly so. What does that make you. . . diet Catholic?"

"No, Episcopalians are diet Catholic. I'm more like a caffeine-free Catholic. I occasionally go to mass because my entire family goes. Our parish has a rainbow flag on the outside, and two of our nuns are married lesbians. I like Jesus' teachings. I don't care for people who strip his words of cultural and historical context for modern political messages. And I'm perfectly fine learning about your craft to better understand exactly what you'll be doing as our paper's Astrology Editor."

Dawn handed me another biscuit.

"Well, then, it sounds like we've got ourselves a nice little bargain."

(Dawn)

My house was quiet save for the occasional bleating of Billie outside. And he was only vocal for a little bit in the morning. The warm smell of coffee filled the kitchen as I fried up an egg sandwich courtesy of the Fates.

A soft clicking noise kicked on as the spout of my coffee maker whirred to life and granted me the caffeine I'd need to start my day.

"Thanks be to Kaldi," I mumbled, pulling out a white mug with a black witch hat and boots painted on the side. Underneath the logo were the words, "Nice shoes. Wanna have hex?"

I grinned as I filled the mug with coffee and watched the steam float up to gently kiss my nose. I didn't add any cream or sugar. They were mainly in my cabinet for guests. Guests like Frankie Dee, who definitely shouldn't be on my mind right now. Because we were professional business partners. Not romantic partners who fell in love after a decidedly amusing one-night stand.

No need to remember how soft her lips were or how she squirmed under my touch. Because there was no way that was happening again.

Yup, I thought, sipping my coffee, picturing things I definitely shouldn't be. *No way.*

I made quick work of my breakfast while scrolling through my social media feeds and replying to a few comments I'd gotten about yesterday's podcast episode.

A few minutes later, I left my phone on my nightstand, donned a simple pair of ripped jeans and a purple tank top, and went into the backyard.

The air was still a bit nippy for a tank top, but I'd be fine once I got used to it. Billie ran up to me as soon as I stepped onto the lawn.

Picking the goat up, I kissed her head gently three times and giggled.

"Okay, my adorable little Billie. I need you to watch the Fates while I say hi to Mother. Can you do that?"

"Baa!" my furry little friend bleated.

"Thatta girl."

I set her down and stepped over the ranch fence and chicken wire into the patch of woods behind my home. Maple and elm trees greeted me with open branches as my bare feet traced over the soil. Taking a deep breath of the cool morning wind, I made my way about 100 feet from my property line to a faerie ring of mushrooms.

Reaching into my pocket, I pulled out a few pieces of candy, unwrapped them, and placed them in the circle.

"Gotta keep the fae happy," I said, grinning. "I certainly don't want them coming for a visit."

A little further into the woods, I found my usual morning meditation spot between two tree stumps. I'd dug out a little hollow in the earth next to a bayberry bush.

Sitting cross-legged, I lowered myself into the little hollow and took a deep breath, closing my eyes. Clearing my mind usually took a few minutes as I typically pictured all the things I had waiting for me ahead in the day to come. But this morning most of my thoughts focussed on a certain newspaper editor. Squinting, I tried to chase them away. The most I managed was to push those thoughts out to the fringe of my subconscious. They were like a herd of ornery goats, and I didn't have a border collie to properly lead them where they needed to go.

"That'll have to do," I mumbled, taking another deep breath, holding it for 10 seconds, and letting it go slowly, feeling my mind sink into the welcome embrace of Mother Gaia as I did every morning.

The feel of soil between my toes, the sound of a blue jay calling out above me, the taste of morning fog that rolled in from Casco Bay. In all of these things, there was magic. I tapped into it and surrendered myself to this beautiful gift of life.

With my body held in place by the roots of this small patch of forest, I opened my spirit to Mother Gaia for a new day of life.

"Mother Gaia, I thank you for the many gifts you provide each day. I greet you by name this morning as I do every day with notes of gratitude on my lips. I sing the song of your beauty with each breath of air released from my lungs. You feed me. You clothe me. You put the very earth under my feet. I receive these blessings and bow my head to the grand start of another new day. May I honor you with it," I prayed aloud to the goddess.

The wind picked up, and I sat there breathing, not in silence, but in the morning sounds of this tiny patch of forest on the west side of Portland. Someone in the next neighborhood over was walking their dog. It barked excitedly at something. In the distance, I heard Billie sound off again. Behind me, a fox darted over one of the stumps and between some tall grass.

My mind drifted to rest as I felt waves of energy from the Earth moving through the ground beneath me and up through the trees.

With a slower breath, I folded into the parcel of nature that held me and remained at peace for a while.

An hour later, I was showered and sitting in my

recording studio down in the basement. Black absorbers hung on each wall around me.

The brown and white carpet muffled my footsteps as I walked over to my laptop and turned everything on. While Adobe Audition booted up and started syncing my files, I walked over to a table behind me and lit some sandalwood incense, softly blowing on the embers to coax wafting smoke to life. It didn't take long before the smell of incense filled my basement studio.

From one of my basement hopper windows, I saw all of the Fates rush by, chasing something. A snake maybe?

Giggling, I took a seat at the computer desk and swung the microphone and its protector around toward me. I cleared my throat and blew my nose.

"Testing 1, 2, 3, 4, 5, 6, 7, 8, testing. Testing," I said, adjusting the levels of my recording.

I pulled a worn notebook with Wednesday Addams on the cover toward me and flipped to the notes I'd made for this episode.

I need to get a new one with Jenna Ortega on the cover, I thought, seeing I only had three or four pages left in this notebook.

Yawning and shaking my head from side to side, I hit the record button and spoke the opening lines of my podcast.

"You're listening to Dawn's Divinations, your #1 witchy podcast for everything from astrology to tarot. On today's episode, I'll be discussing tips for grounding yourself against chaotic energy, what's up with Jupiter lately, and I have a recorded interview with Maria Gonzalez about her newest book on shadow work and what we all get wrong when trying to tackle it."

Pausing for a moment, I took a breath away from my microphone and a quick sip of water.

"But before we get into all that, I want to take a minute to thank the sponsor for today's episode, Bombo Socks. When I'm hiking in Acadia National Park and trying to connect with nature, it's so much easier to get my head right when I'm wearing socks that keep my feet dry and cool no matter the weather. Bombo Socks have a variety of materials, all ethically sourced and made by hand for any of your comfort needs, whether you're hiking down a trail or recording a witchy podcast episode."

I spent the rest of the morning recording, editing, and proofing the latest episode before submitting it to my distributor that would push it across to various digital platforms where my listeners were subscribed to me. When I'd finished adding a few bonus recordings for my Patreon subscribers, I got up and stretched.

"Oh goddess, I'm tired," I said.

Right about that time, my stomach let me know that the egg sandwich I'd eaten a few hours ago was depleted. And it hungered for more.

"Easy, tum tum. You're growling louder than I

did while reading the things Gretchen said to Imogen in the restaurant."

As I tried to figure out what I could make for lunch with rice, flour, and breadcrumbs, I reminded myself to go grocery shopping tonight. Just like I'd reminded myself last night before playing two hours of *Little Kitty, Big City*.

My phone buzzed, and I found a text from Keyla waiting for me as I unlocked the screen.

"Client canceled meeting. Lunch?" she wrote.

As I grinned and confirmed our lunch date, I practically ran into my room to throw on a purple v-neck shirt, a black broom skirt, and a long flowing jacket I left unbuttoned.

Keyla worked at a little accounting office in Knightville, so I made the 15-minute drive along the Fore River and over the Casco Bay Bridge. I always liked Knightville. It was quiet and had such pretty views of Portland's harbor from Thomas Knight Park. You could walk up a little ramp to a platform halfway between the Casco Bay Bridge and the water, and the harbor would hide no secrets from you on a sunny day. Cruise ships that docked in town, sailboats, and cargo vessels having their shipping containers unloaded via crane, you could see it all. And a little further in the distance, you could spot some of the taller buildings in downtown Portland like the M&T Bank Building and the Time and Temperature Building flashing words like "Call Joe."

Half of Knightville seemed like a little residential cluster just across the water from Maine's biggest city, and half of it seemed like a little downtown section for SoPo.

Sitting right smack dab in the middle of the little neighborhood was a Mexican restaurant called Taco Duo.

I walked inside to the smell of salsa and cooking beef, instantly reminding me how hungry I was. Working while hungry. Who did that remind me of? A certain newspaper editor I definitely wasn't still thinking about now that my podcast was finished and uploaded.

Sitting at an orange table surrounded by blue and yellow chairs, I spotted perhaps the only real friend I'd made since moving to Maine. She was munching on chips and salsa frowning at her phone as I walked over.

"Hey girl!" she said, standing up and throwing her arms around me. I smiled and returned Keyla's crushing hug.

"Well, that's a much happier look than the one you had five seconds ago. Did another coworker ask why you spelled your name 'weird' again?" I asked as we both sat down.

Neither of us needed a menu. We'd both eaten here enough to have the damn thing memorized in English and Spanish.

Keyla rolled her eyes.

"Not quite. Thankfully, I have nothing new to

report from the accounting firm of Snow and Cream. But I did make my boss squirm last week by asking what the office's plans for celebrating Juneteenth this year were. That man set a land speed record for sweat. His shirt was soaked in about 20 seconds," she said, giggling.

I snickered.

Sitting across from me was a tall, gorgeous Black woman wearing a nice blouse and slacks. She looked every part the role of an accountant. But seeing as Maine was literally the whitest state in the U.S., Keyla didn't exactly look like a carbon copy of her coworkers, most of whom were middle-aged white men who drove nice trucks or SUVs to the office.

If Keyla didn't draw the occasional glance for her skin color, she might be stared at for her shaved head. It was the typical fuckery people of color dealt with existing in a society we'd constructed primarily for people who looked like me.

We both met on the Merrill Theatre Fundraising Committee, a group of five people who help plan how best to take money from people to keep a beautiful and underfunded fine arts location from being shuttered and bulldozed for luxury condos or some bullshit.

"No, I was scowling because I haven't been able to find any resources for dating, uh, trans men," Keyla said, putting her phone in her purse.

I flashed her a wicked grin.

"Oh? Got yourself a new boyfriend, Keyla? And why haven't I seen any pictures or even heard this man's name? You've been holding out on me!"

My best friend in the entire world rolled her eyes for a second time, and we got up to order our food. Before long, she had a chorizo burrito, and I had a plate of mole enchiladas with beans and rice.

Between mouthfuls of delicious food, I poked at Keyla's dating life again.

"So. . . his name?"

She looked up and finished a bite before answering.

"His name is Lalo. We go to the same gym. He's been helping me with weightlifting and eventually asked for my number."

My smile only grew.

"Yeah. . . and?"

She sneered.

"Bitch, shut up. It ain't like that. . . not yet, anyway."

"There it is!" I almost whooped.

She jabbed a finger in my face.

"You shut that mouth, or I'll turn you over to the Church and tell them you're secretly a witch. They'll give you the rack or something."

"Keyla, I already have a perfectly functional rack."

She raised an eyebrow but couldn't keep from snickering.

"And tell me. . . has anybody made good use of

it lately? I mean — it's been two months since Jessica dumped you, right? How do you know your tits are still perfectly functional?"

I stared down at the table and found myself at a loss for words. I was thinking about Frankie Dee again and the feeling of her breasts pressed against mine. The way they — fuck! The goal was to keep things professional. And I couldn't do that if I kept wishing she'd get under me again (and stay awake this time).

"Oh my god, you're picturing someone right now, aren't you? Who is she? Tell me her name."

"Oh no no, my friend. You first. Tell me about Lalo," I said, taking another bite of my enchilada.

Keyla scratched her cheek and then looked at her plate, not eating.

"He's really cute, got a body that looks like it was chiseled by a Renaissance sculptor."

I cocked my head to the side as a husband and wife got up from the table beside us to leave and head home.

"Then what's the issue? It sounds like you're attracted to him."

"I am! He's great. And he makes me laugh. The other day we were passing a truck that had a license plate with the letters F-O-O-F-O-O on it. He said, 'Huh. Must belong to a bunny.'"

I just stared at my bestie and started to reevaluate my friend options. It only took me three years to make a real friend in Maine. I bet I could shorten the next friend search to two years.

"That's not funny, Keyla. That's just sad."

She smiled.

"Okay, so his jokes aren't funny. But Lalo THINKS he's funny. And I find that shit hilarious. I just. . . I've never dated a trans man before, and I want to make sure I don't accidentally say something insensitive, ya know? I fully accept he's a man. He's a man's man. And bonus, Lalo was raised without any macho bullshit or toxic masculinity."

I just ate quietly while I listened.

"I like him plenty. And him trusting me with that secret before we even went on an official date took guts. I just want to make sure I'm being respectful and returning that courtesy," she said.

Reaching across the table, I took her hand. She looked up, and I smiled.

"I think you're going to be perfectly fine, Keyla. Just treat him like any other guy you've dated. Minus Robert, because that poor dude is probably still in therapy after what you did to him."

She scowled.

"That fucker knows what he did and absolutely had it coming."

I threw up my hands in surrender.

One of the cashiers stared at us and shook his head before walking back into the kitchen. My eyes wandered around to the painted yellow walls of the restaurant, walls lined with double lights, stenciled flowers, and framed art.

Keyla's burrito had officially broken into pieces, so she'd transitioned to finishing the insides with a spoon. I watched as she scooped up pork and potatoes.

"So, tell me about this girl," Keyla said, narrowing her eyes.

I sighed.

"What's to tell? She's managing editor of the Portland Lighthouse-Journal, the same paper I just signed a contract with to become their Horoscope Editor," I said. "Frankie told me she wants to keep things professional."

Keyla drooped a little, almost like she was feeling sorry for me. Hell, with how badly I wanted to do things to Frankie Dee, I felt sorry for me.

"Of course, this was after I took Frankie home semi-drunk from a book club meeting, and we fooled around," I mumbled, taking a drink of my tea.

My bestie's eyes widened, and she pointed a finger in my face again.

"I think you should have started your story there, Dawn. Jesus. I believe your new coworker would call that 'burying the lede.' You took your future coworker home from a bar, and she asked to keep things professional afterward?"

A little boy with a skateboard came in and

picked up his to-go order, only to be scolded by an employee for trying to skate between tables on the way out.

"There's nuance! Context! Geez. Neither of us knew who we were. It was her first time at the book club meeting, and we'd only previously talked over email," I said, finishing my enchiladas.

"So. . . you didn't know. Damn, Dawn. You sure do like your complicated romances," Keyla said, rubbing the back of her neck. "So what are you doing to do?"

I shrugged.

"What can I do?" I said, with my elbows on the table. "There are times when she looks at me where I can practically hear her begging me to hold her. It's like. . . she's being crushed by this boulder, and I'm the first person to walk by in days. And the way she takes me seriously and asks real questions about my craft, it just. . .," I trailed off.

My heart quivered hearing her ask me questions about Artemis and The Morrigan again. I wanted her to see more of me. Gods! I wanted her to know every inch of me, body and soul. Midnight and magic.

Looking up at Keyla, I sighed.

"She sees me, Keyla. And I suspect she doesn't want to keep things professional. I think she's secretly hoping I'll push at the door until she's left with no choice but to open it and press our lips together. But until she says that. . . I can't know for sure."

The accountant across from me raised an eyebrow and shook her head.

"Damn, bitch. You got it down bad."

My phone vibrated.

Looking at the screen, my heart started racing for an entirely different reason. And for a moment, all I could hear was a man shouting from the pulpit and smell the odor of an old carpet. I could taste the wafers and grape juice. Somewhere in the back of my head, Mom's voice said, "I was wrong. Run."

"So what are you going to do?" Keyla asked.

I just shook my head staring at the name "Ex-Father (Shitbag)" on my phone's screen. My heart thumped even harder in my chest as I declined the call and fought to keep from screaming, "Leave me alone!"

Amid all the panic, I felt Keyla's hand on my arm.

"Dawn? Are you okay?"

I put my phone back in my purse and wiped my forehead.

"Yeah! Yeah. . . sorry. Just kind of zoned out there for a moment. What were we talking about again?"

The restaurant's phone rang behind me as a customer called in an order.

"I asked what you were going to do about this

Frankie girl, and you got really pale really fast," she said.

Shrugging, all I could say was, "I don't know what I'm going to do."

What *was* I going to do?

7

(Frankie)

The newsroom was quiet at 5:30 p.m., which was a little strange on a Friday evening. Usually, the Friday news dump would have our reporters scrambling on at least one or two stories. We'd expected our governor to announce her decision on a new offshore wind farm application today, and she'd so far sent nothing.

If Brian isn't responding to my texts there must still be some last-minute meetings going on in Augusta, I thought. Brian Tildry was the governor's executive assistant and my best source for news tips when it came to Maine's executive branch.

I walked over to our breakroom, opened Apple Pay, and got a bag of chips from the vending machine.

Salt and caffeine are a journalist's two best friends, I thought as I started to feel woozy for the second time today.

Right as I started to open my chips, our IT person walked into the room and all but cornered me. The smell of cigarettes and hand sanitizer filled the air.

"Frankie Dee, do you know what happens when you don't respond to my text messages?"

Sighing and lowering my dinner from my taste buds, who were about to start a revolution at being denied a salty snack, I scanned our super short computer engineer. "Fun-sized," I occasionally called them.

Their name was Ghost, and they looked every bit the part. Pale skin, undercut, hair dyed white, and colored contact lenses that made their irises the color of flour. Ghost's nails were painted gunmetal grey, and it was difficult not to stare at their tongue piercing every now and again.

But they were a fucking wizard on a keyboard and didn't give me too much shit about not being able to pay as well as news outlets in Boston's market.

"I'm sorry, Ghost. I've been on a Zoom call for the last hour with a new applicant for our printing press apprenticeship. I didn't even have time to glance at my phone," I said.

After rolling their eyes, the IT expert said, "You know, when you're using your phone for a Zoom call, you can respond to iMessages on your laptop, right? That's why I set that up for you two months ago."

Rubbing my temples, I apologized again.

"Because when you don't respond to my texts asking me what time I can take our servers offline for maintenance tonight, I have to leave my den and come find you. Do you know what happens when I leave my den?"

I shook my head.

"People talk to me! Emma wanted to see my Cowboy Bebop tattoo, Richard asked if his computer had a virus (it didn't), and Craig wanted me to listen to some new song from an Australian DJ. I don't have the spoons to be a social butterfly, Frankie," Ghost said.

I fought a grin. Our IT expert was. . . not the most social person around. They preferred to stay in their office, and if you had a tech problem, you were supposed to email them. Don't call them. Don't holler for them. And definitely don't knock on their door.

We called their office a den because it was an icebox to keep the servers cool, the lights were usually off, and Ghost did not like to leave it. Hell, some days I didn't even see Ghost in person.

They were the only staff member with access to this building's basement, and they used it to come in and out of the news office unseen. I almost respected that level of antisocial dedication.

"I'd hardly call three conversations totaling less than 45 seconds much of a social outing, Ghost," I snickered.

And they honest to god hissed.

"Answer. My. Texts. Please."

"Um, do I text you back now, or can I just tell you face-to-face?"

"Well, I'm already here, so you might as well tell me in person. I swear to god, I'm going to take that job in Montreal," they muttered.

I stifled another giggle. Some people thought Ghost was a little prickly. And they absolutely were. But I always got a kick out of their quirks and did my best to be accommodating.

"Midnight should be fine? I think our web traffic tends to drop off then for the night," I said, rubbing my chin.

They nodded and turned to leave.

"Well, you certainly smoke enough to fit in with the other Québécois, but how is your French?"

I watched our IT expert leave the room shortly before calling back, "Je t'emmerde."

I'll look that up later, I thought, knowing I absolutely wouldn't.

The refrigerator in the breakroom started to hum and rattle as I stared at the yellow-ing appliance. Don't get me wrong. We kept the inside immaculately clean. But she was approaching 30 years running. We didn't have the money in our newsroom budget to replace it. Just another piece of technology we kept operating with engine grease and chewing gum. It matched the outdated blue and white cabinets that squeaked no matter what angle you opened them from.

My shoes also squeaked as I walked across the white tile floor and finally started to eat my chips.

I was half-finished with my dinner when I returned to my office and found Dawn waiting for me. The sight of her pleasant curves and sparkling emerald eyes spun my heart faster than a Beyblade.

"H — hi, Dawn."

"The dinner of champions?" she asked, standing up and placing both hands on her hips. Hips I truly missed feeling against mine.

C'mon, now. Professional, Frankie. Keep things professional, I thought, pushing those feelings away as best I could.

Before I could answer, the witch walked forward, snatched the bag of chips from my hand, and folded it over, placing it on my desk.

"I know I don't need to remind you of this, but dessert comes AFTER dinner, Frankie," she said, gently pushing me toward the door after grabbing my small leather purse.

All I could do was gasp.

"Hey now!" I protested, but surprisingly, none of my employees came to my defense. In fact, I'm pretty sure Emma was audibly laughing.

When we got outside, I anchored myself as best I could.

"Where are you taking me?"

She raised an eyebrow.

"To get a proper dinner. Because I'm assuming the last real meal you had before those chips was a bowl of cereal this morning," she said.

I crossed my arms.

"Frankie Dee, you've been in this office for — what — 12 hours today? Let's take a fucking dinner break."

When I cocked my head to the side, she added, "As colleagues, not girlfriends. Geez. Lighten up. Coworkers get lunch together all the time. We can keep it professional. We don't even need to trade chapstick."

With a slight wink, the witch left me paralyzed. The warmth of her cinnamon breath and the brush of her painted lips against mine like an artist shading a canvas was a potent memory. As I froze, Dawn giggled and again softly moved me down the sidewalk.

We wound up walking down Congress Street a few blocks to the Munjoy Hill Inn, a tall and narrow building, its first story made of brick, and everything above that faded white siding. Seagulls screamed above us, and out of the corner of my eye, I saw one shit on a cyclist who nearly lost control of their bike and swerved madly to the left.

He cursed and stopped to wipe his arm clean with a napkin from his pocket.

That was the thing about Portland's seagulls.

You never knew when they were going to dump on you. I remember standing in line waiting for ice cream on a hot summer day when one shit on my shoulder, and some of it got into my hair.

Fucking birds, I thought, shaking my head, remembering how I swore the entire walk home, all during the shower, and on the jog back to the newsroom.

My foot scraped against the concrete on the sidewalk's edge, jarring me back to reality.

"Ope, easy there. You good? Looked like you tried to slip off the curb," Dawn said, grabbing my arm before I faceplanted on Congress Street. "Let's get you some proper dinner before you collapse."

The witch opened a single heavy wooden door and motioned for me to head inside. I said nothing, having eaten more than a few meals here. It was actually one of Dad's favorite spots. He brought me here as a kid all the time for meal breaks. He was better about eating than I was.

The interior of Munjoy Hill Inn was mostly exposed brick and chalkboards on the wall detailing drink selections and menu choices in plenty of colorful sketchings.

Dawn found us a table next to the long wooden bar where a woman wearing a yellow button-down shirt and a blue jacket was shaking a cocktail in a mixer.

The bartender made her way over to our table as the restaurant started to fill for the evening dinner rush. I ordered a personal pan pizza and garlic bread, to which, Dawn suggested I add a bowl of greens. She ordered a turkey sandwich.

"At least try to get a few vegetables with dinner, won't you?" she asked as the bartender took our menus.

I scoffed.

"I'm getting onions on my pizza. Thanks, MOM," I said, slumping in my chair and adding a side salad to my meal. This fucking witch, I swear.

"What are you bitching about? I didn't say anything about your garlic bread, did I?"

I started to retort but was interrupted by the witch reaching into her purse and grabbing something to tie around my wrist.

Before I could ask what she was doing, the witch had her hands back on her side of the table, and a tumbled gemstone was secured to my wrist with thin, black leather straps.

"What is this?" I asked, pointing to the polished black stone.

"Tourmaline. It absorbs negative energy. I'm hoping it'll reduce your grumpiness about being forced to eat veggies with dinner. Is it working?" she asked.

I didn't want to do her the favor of admitting I did strangely feel a little better with this rock tied to my wrist. And it was very pretty, like an oil slick, but with more of an artistic flair.

Behind us, a group of guys cheered at the Blue

Sox game playing on a mounted TV. One nearly spilled his beer shouting something about a "hell of a pitch."

"It's pretty," I confessed. "But is it professional?"

She shrugged.

"If you don't want it, give it back."

I clutched my wrist and pulled back with a frown.

"No."

Dawn leaned over the table, her shadow covering the ciders we'd ordered, and she said, "Then it's professional."

Scoffing, I drowned any snide remark I had left lingering in the booze.

Our food came, and I found myself more ravished than expected. The garlic bread and pizza, I inhaled like a plate of cookies in front of a pink starfish. And the greens? Child's play. I ate them faster than Billie could've.

I immediately placed a second order for two more sides of garlic bread while Dawn giggled into her sandwich.

"See what happens when you actually eat? You feel better," she said.

Finishing my cider, I found myself staring at the bracelet again. Its weight on my wrist felt. . . reassuring somehow. It felt like someone made a small effort to protect me from the whirlpool I was struggling to avoid being swallowed by each day.

"I got our loan request back from Gorham First Security Bank," I mumbled.

Dawn raised an eyebrow.

"They declined since we're already paying back another business loan to Portland Community Credit Union. And my father only got that loan because he's golf buddies with the president of that particular financial branch."

With a long deep sigh, I suddenly felt more vulnerable and yet relaxed than I had in a long time. Maybe it was having a warm meal in my belly. Perhaps it was the liquor. Or it could've been the charming witch sitting across from me who made me want to spill every little secret tucked away in my heart. I swear, she could coax every lock in Fort Knox to retire with a gentle smile.

"I don't mean to add any pressure, but if your horoscope section launch could bring in a few more thousand subscribers, it'd be pretty great," I said, staring out the window at a woman walking her golden retriever down the sidewalk.

Dawn placed a hand on mine.

"This newspaper is going to be the death of me," I mumbled without thinking. And the witch's eyes widened.

"Hey, we don't have to talk about work, you know? We can talk about literally anything else."

I devoured another piece of garlic bread, feeling the buttery goodness bring a little bit of relief to my sudden downpour of spirit. I wasn't sure I wanted to ever get up from this table. Every weight in my body decided to drop anchor here tonight, and dammit if I lacked the confidence to shake it off.

"I've got one. If you could date any fictional witch, who would it be?" Dawn asked, finishing her sandwich.

The question caught me off guard, and I shook my head, mind rising from the river current that'd been dragging it down for the last few minutes.

"Excuse me?" I asked.

"What? You're obviously not going to date me because of ethics or some shit. So pick a fictional witch who doesn't work for you to take on a date. Who do you choose?"

A small Swanson-sized giggle escaped my throat as I considered the possibilities. This was an outrageous question. I dealt with facts. Indisputable data and information that my subscribers trusted me to deliver to them in a timely manner.

"Does Raven from the Teen Titans count? Her grown-up version? I'm pretty sure she was a witch."

That earned me a small sympathetic smile from the new Horoscope Editor.

"More like an intergalactic telepath. Try again, FeeDee."

I ignored her use of the wrong name and pictured another group.

"Oh! Those girls from Scooby Doo. You know — the ones in the band?"

Dawn let loose a bellowing laugh that caught

the attention of our baseball neighbors as they stared for a few seconds. When she got wind back in her lungs, she said, "The Hex Girls?"

"Yeah! The Hex Girls."

My dinner partner nodded and stole a piece of garlic bread, tearing off a small bite before putting it back in the wicker basket.

"Okay, The Hex Girls. All of them?"

"Why not?" I asked. "Any or all. They could put a spell on me."

That mischievous grin worked its way back onto the witch's face, the dangerous one that lured me to her house. . . and couch. . . and bed. I stifled a quick gasp. She definitely noticed but said nothing.

"How about you?" I asked. "Who would you pick?"

Without hesitation, Dawn said, "Oh, Bonnie Bennett for sure."

"From 'Vampire Diaries'?" I asked.

Dawn nodded with a satisfied smile on her face.

"She was so badass. I'd fight Enzo for her any day," the witch said as my phone vibrated. I checked a text, and it actually turned out to be a picture from one of my friends, a journalism professor at South Portland Community College, which sat right on the shoreline.

There was a fire. A large white boat with yellow paint down the side.

Shit, I thought, zooming in and realizing it was a

ferry. She'd snapped the photo from the Spring Point Ledge Lighthouse. *That's the Bug Light Ferry.*

Standing up with every muscle in my body and mind starting to protest, I felt my hands shaking.

Come on, Frankie! I thought. *This is breaking news. You've done this thousands of times! Get to work.*

But my chest was starting to ache and throb. My legs wanted to give out and sit back down as weakness filled me.

"What's wrong?" Dawn asked with more concern in her voice than coworkers typically give each other.

"There's a fire on one of the ferries that goes out to Peaks Island. I gotta get back to the newsroom," I said, grabbing the table for support.

More pain radiated from my chest, and I took short breaths, closing my eyes and willing it away. It didn't work very well.

"Why don't you sit down? Text Emma or something. Isn't this why you have an evening city editor?"

I shook my head.

"I mean — yes. That's why I do. But what good is a managing editor who isn't in the trenches with her reporters? They respect me because I'm always willing to hop in wherever there's a gap. Covering meetings, writing stories, proofreading, and even taking pictures. I do it all, and this is going to be an all-hands-on-deck night."

Dawn furrowed her brow.

"You're awfully pale, Frankie. And you've already put in 12 hours today. I can see your legs shaking from here. Why don't you sit back down, and I'll give you a ride home? Seriously, I'm worried."

My heart was at war. On one front, I was demanding it give me the strength to power through an evening of breaking news. On another, it swooned over someone actually telling me to give it a rest for once. And not just anyone. . . but the girl I'd give anything to stop being professional with.

The bartender came over with our ticket, and I put some cash on the table.

"Keep the change," I said, turning to go and nearly colliding with one of the baseball bros. He steadied me, and I apologized.

Dawn was quickly beside me as I called Craig.

"Where are you?" I asked, as soon as he picked up.

"City Hall. They're about to meet and vote on —" I interrupted him.

"Scrap it. Take your camera and head to Bug Light. There's a ferry on fire, and I want pictures. Use the big lens. Hustle over there, but take your time with the photos. It's getting darker, so you'll need to keep the camera more steady to get clear shots."

"You got it, Boss," he said.

I sighed and walked outside, nearly spilling into

the street again. What was it with my legs and this particular section of sidewalk? Fuck.

"Don't call me that," I said, hanging up and immediately calling Emma.

She answered, and I fired off a list of things to do, telling her I was on my way back to the newsroom.

"Call the PIO for the US Coast Guard Station in SoPo. He doesn't answer after hours, but he will check his voicemail through the night, so leave him a message. I'm going to text a contact who works in the dispatch office for the Bug Light Ferry system."

"Yes ma'am," Emma said, hanging up.

My chest throbbed even harder as I walked uphill toward the newsroom. Dawn tried one final time to convince me to let my night crew handle this.

"I truly think you should rest, Frankie. You're sweating and really pale."

Huffing, I walked and talked.

"Seventy-five years the Portland Lighthouse-Journal has served as the leading source of news for Maine's biggest city. Equity firms want to buy us out. Subscribers call and ask why they need us when they can get their news for free on Facebook. And the TV stations try to take our content at least three times a month. But we're still here. A Ricci at the helm of this paper keeping the public informed is what's kept us afloat for 75 years. And I can't quit now, Dawn. I won't. These are the moments they need us, and I refuse to let our readers down."

My hand clutched the doorknob of our office, and I took a steadying breath. It was going to be a long night of breaking news push alerts, redoing the front page layout, evening press conferences, and hopefully, news that everyone made it back to shore alive.

I'd be there to cover it all with my team, chest pain be damned.

8

(Dawn)

Our boots crunched over dirt and twigs as Frankie Dee and I made our way to the northeast side of Mackworth Island. Seagulls screamed above us in the last couple hours of daylight while crows darted under trees and out of their sight.

I didn't have much trouble feeding crows over in Brighton Corner a little farther from the shore. But trying to feed them on the peninsula was much more difficult. If seagulls saw even a tiny piece of food, and you weren't actively giving it to them, they'd swoop in and take it.

And I don't know if you've ever seen a seagull in person, but they're fucking huge. They won't just take your lunch. They'll take your lunch money AND give you a swirlie if it's high tide.

Frankie said nothing as she hopped over a log. I felt at peace with her beside me, almost like we were two little girls wandering through the woods looking for a spot to build a fort before our parents called us home for dinner.

At least Frankie can go home and have a nice dinner with her parents, I thought. *All my father wanted to do was berate me for "poor life choices."*

But fuck him. I'd gone no contact when I moved to Maine, and while I was a little lonely during the first couple of years here, my life had been immensely better.

The newspaper editor had her blonde hair pulled back in a tight braid the ocean breeze had no trouble whipping this way and that.

"Okay, so remind me what we're doing out here again?" Frankie Dee asked, not with a tone of boredom or skepticism, just plain curiosity.

"Well, for starters, I fought to pull you out of the newsroom at 6 p.m. because normal people don't work 12-14 hour shifts every single day."

She rolled her eyes, but the newspaper editor actually took a sick day after pulling an all-nighter covering the ferry fire with her staff. The poor girl could barely move as I drove her home the next morning at 4 a.m.

Thankfully, because of highly-trained professionals, the ferry had been evacuated and towed to a private dock for repairs.

Only one person was hospitalized, and it was for smoke inhalation, according to Craig's front-page article, which I read the next morning while baking muffins, muffins I took to a certain bedridden newspaper editor who was still doing some work on a laptop before sleep took her like a villain in a Liam Neeson flick.

"Hey, I typically only work a few hours on Sunday," she said.

"Six hours is not a 'few,' Frankie Dee," I said as another gull flew over.

She shook her head and turned away to hide a smile. But I saw it because I'm nothing if not an observant. . . colleague.

"Let me try again. Why did you ask me to meet you here on Mackworth Island?" she asked.

"Why, to honor our bargain, of course," I said with a wide grin. Unlike Frankie, I didn't bother to hide my smile. I wanted her to know I was a mischievous little witch.

My companion paused to lean against a tree that was starting to show signs of growing back its leaves for spring.

"Remind me about the supposed bargain we made again?" she asked with a small smirk.

"You teach me about journalism, and I teach you about witchcraft," I said, continuing down the trail.

The smell of low tide overtook the island as scents of saltwater and seaweed filled the air. Some folks couldn't stand it, but it always felt raw to me, an immutable aspect of nature that mankind couldn't ignore or send away. It was the ocean saying, "I've been here for billions of years. This is what I smell like sometimes. And if you don't like it, you can move to fucking Iowa."

A fate worse than death, I thought, remembering the endless cornfields stretched out across the horizon. And if it wasn't corn, it was soybeans. On and on the sea of brown and green went, this ocean carrying scents of chicken houses and granaries.

We passed a bush trying to reclaim its clothes for the warming season before walking down a set of old concrete stairs onto a narrow beach.

"Your column on how celestial bodies have impacted human nature for millennia was wicked cool," Frankie said. "I didn't expect so much history as you moved through how people have relied on stars for everything from chronology to navigation across the ages."

"Thank you," I said, clearing my throat to stifle a tiny sob.

Not only did she read my first column, I thought. *But she analyzed and thought about it.*

Her compliment wasn't empty or meant to merely serve as a passing kindness. My coworker had actually found interest in my craft, and that stirred something in me. Something that wanted. . . more. Of course, I'd spent the first week knowing Frankie and wanting more from her physically. But now? I wanted her attention and affection. I wanted her thoughts. I wanted her to know me the way nobody else did, the way nobody else cared to.

Professional boundaries be damned. . . if she wanted.

"And what aspect of witchcraft are you going to teach me about today?" she asked as we passed a sign.

I merely held my arms wide pointing to several handmade structures of sticks and stone overlooking the beach before saying, "Faeries."

Her eyes widened, and she stood frozen, processing my word choice while I read a small white and green sign posted nearby that said, "Welcome to Mackworth Island Community Village."

It continued, "You may build houses small and hidden for the faeries, but please do not use living or artificial materials. The best materials are found in the landscape of the village itself, but if you choose to bring in natural materials, please return with those that you didn't use. Thank you for treating this island with care and respect. This helps keep the faeries coming back."

Frankie opened her mouth twice and closed it, trying to decide what she'd say.

Finally, she just settled on, "Faeries?"

I liked that. She wasn't trying to offend. The newspaper editor simply wanted to understand. Because what else can you do when someone says they want to teach you about fae? Images of Tinkerbell or *A Midsummer Night's Dream* came to mind, little pixies or people being turned into animals.

This was the difference between someone saying they wanted to teach you about gravity and someone saying they wanted to teach you about unicorns. One of those subjects was taught by people like Bill Nye and Carl Sagan. The other was taught by a spectrum that ranged from Hasbro to Peter S. Beagle.

To her credit, Frankie Dee seemed to recover and crossed her arms.

"Okay, where do we start?" she asked.

That warmth flickered in my chest again. She wasn't cracking jokes or laughing at my expense. The girl I was down bad for legit seemed ready to learn. . . about fae of all things. So, I took a deep breath and asked, "What do you know about Mackworth Island?"

Without much hesitation, Frankie replied, "It's home to a school for the deaf, and the whole place is a state park."

I walked over to what looked like a poor attempt at a log cabin made of twigs and small branches. Some seashells and leaves made up the roof. In all, the little structure was about the size of a basketball. I motioned for Frankie to come closer.

"Mackworth Island is also home to a rich tradition of making faerie houses, natural homes for tiny elves who sometimes visit our world."

Frankie looked inside and didn't seem surprised to find the faerie house empty.

"Are you going to get mad at me if I ask what I'm supposed to be looking for?" she asked.

I shook my head.

"What I'd tell you is that you aren't supposed to be looking for anything. Because the Fair Folk don't like to be seen. They might steal a sock from your hanging laundry. They could bless your bread to never grow stale. They may even place a shiny trinket in a faerie circle in hopes of ensnaring any human dumb enough to pick it up. But you'll probably never see them," I said.

Frankie looked inside the little house again and nodded. Then she straightened her back and stretched, looking out at the water.

An American Airlines jet flew over Casco Bay, making an approach toward the Fore River and presumably the Portland Jetport. I watched the newspaper editor nod slowly and wet her lips. Behind her, a sailboat drifted toward Great Diamond Island.

May had officially begun, and some days were growing warmer, while the nights quickly reclaimed their chill after the sun went down. Today, the golden ball in the sky was clear and bright with temperatures that would've been warm enough to carry the promise of spring. That is. . . if it weren't for that brisk northern wind saying, "Hold your horses. Winter takes her time to cede Maine to summer."

Frankie Dee cracked her knuckles and asked, "So, what's the deeper lesson here?"

I cleared my throat and moistened my lips.

"That I'm a cute and fun person to spend the evening with," I said, running my hands down my hips.

My companion froze, and I watched Frankie's cheeks turn nice and rosy as she spun to look out at the water and recover herself.

Without turning back to me, she found her voice, albeit shaky, and said, "That's not much of a lesson, Dawn. I already knew those things the night you took me home. Er — to your home. What's the deeper lesson as it relates to witchcraft?"

She finally faced me again.

My smirk hadn't budged an inch.

"Ah. Well, then the deeper lesson here is that witchcraft isn't about what you can see. It's about what you learn from old stories passed down through generations, from literature, and from people who love you. And it's about the things felt while walking your path in life. You're Catholic. Isn't there something about not relying on sight in that holy book of yours? Don't you believe in things you can't see?"

Those last two questions seemed to bring Frankie out of her thoughts. She took a breath before answering.

"Fair. Yes, I think that verse is in Hebrews. Something about the evidence of things not seen. I take your point about believing in things I can't see. I think every person has a guardian angel that looks out for them. When my dad was having his heart attack, I believe his guardian angel stayed with him and gave him the strength to persevere until he got to the operating table. If that's possible, why not faeries? Er — fae? Which word should I use?"

I shrugged.

"Whichever. I don't think Holly Black is going to hunt you down for using one word or another," I said, starting to gather some longer sticks. "And I'm glad your dad made it. Mr. Ricci has some great stories. Like how when you were seven, you carried a notebook everywhere and interviewed every single person you saw because you wanted to be like him."

Covering her face with her hands, my companion groaned and kicked at the sand. She knocked a rock down into an advancing wave, causing a small splash.

"Noooooooo. Fuck. He's already telling you stories about me?" Frankie Dee grimaced. "You've gotta do me a favor, bub. Stop encouraging him. I keep trying to get him to take up golfing or sitting at Applebee's or whatever the hell old white men do, but he insists the paper's publisher needs to be in the newsroom, apparently telling embarrassing tales instead of Lighthouse-Journal history."

With a giggle, I said, "What? I think it's cute. He's obviously very proud of you. Just like I'm sure he was back then when you reported on important things like the price of milk cartons increasing by a nickel at preschool."

That seemed to strike a nerve. An adorable nerve.

"Fuck you," Frankie said. "Consider your column canceled along with the rest of your witch lessons."

I laughed all the harder.

A few minutes later, I was carving a little trench in the ground a few feet away from a large rock about half my height. Then, I placed the branches and sticks into the trench and leaned them against the boulder to make a rough wall.

"It's your first faerie house, so I figure we'll keep it basic. A simple lean-to should suffice."

While I established the outer wall, Frankie got down on her knees and cleared out the inside of leaves and pebbles until there was nothing but a neat dirt floor she stamped down with a flat rock. I couldn't help but notice she was still wearing the bracelet I'd given her, which made me smile. In yet another way, it seemed like the newspaper editor was taking my beliefs seriously.

I found some long blades of grass nearby and put a second layer on the stick wall, tying the grass horizontally across the branches I leaned against the boulder. Meanwhile, Frankie found a wide cap of a mushroom, picked it, flipped it over, and carved out the gills. This left a bowl-shaped piece of fungus she filled with moss picked from a nearby log.

Frankie placed the little bed inside the house, and I nodded.

"Nice. You sure did pick this up quickly," I said.

"Well, it's actually pretty fun. I'm glad you invited me out here. So. . . the little elf that stays here will have a shelter and a soft bed. What else are we missing?" Frankie asked, standing up and popping her back.

I reached into my purse and pulled out a bag of sunflower seeds I'd picked up from the gas station near my home.

"An offering, of course," I said, emptying half the package of seeds in front of the tiny bed my companion had made.

"So. . . what? You're bribing the faerie that stays here to bless your bread?"

Shrugging again, I said, "Or to simply leave me off the list of humans they intend to prank next week. You never know. Fae are unpredictable folk. I find it's best to simply make your offering and go about your business."

On the beach, I found a chunk of orange feldspar with deep vertical grooves worn into its pattern. Frankie watched me pocket the stone after wiping all the sand off it.

"That's a pretty little gem," she said.

I nodded, pulling out a smooth piece of granite

I'd found in the woods behind my house and setting it down in the sand.

The newspaper editor just looked at me with a raised eyebrow.

Running my fingers over the feldspar in my pocket, I said, "Oh, the fae never give anything away for free. So if I find a pretty stone here, I always leave one from the forest behind my house as a trade. You NEVER want to owe a fae debt."

Frankie rubbed her chin and looked down at the rock I'd placed on the beach.

"These fae sure do have a lot of rules," she said. I waited for a grin or some kind of smirk, any indication that she was making fun of me or not taking this seriously. All I saw was a thoughtful expression, like Frankie was visualizing a notebook in her head and a floating pen writing down every faerie fact I gave her.

The joy in my chest only grew as she continued thinking and then turned in my direction with a smile. Butterflies in my stomach made me want to leave a note inside the little faerie house we'd built.

It would read, "Dear whoever finds this, Should you find time to help a pitiful lovesick mortal, I could use your assistance in gently persuading my coworker to dissolve our professional boundaries and stick her tongue down my throat. Thanks, your friendly Portland witch, Dawn." I wouldn't leave my last name because you never give any creature or being your full name. That only invites trouble from those who would have more influence over your fate.

With my mind turning back to rules, I said, "Fae are strangely obsessed with rules for being such chaotic spirits of nature. They love to follow the letter of their laws while dancing through loopholes and double meanings."

Nodding, Frankie just added, "Hard tellin' not knowin', I suppose."

Right about that time, I heard the flutter of wings and the call of a familiar black bird in the ash tree above us. The sun was getting lower, and temperatures were dropping. But this was the time my friend usually appeared.

"Well, hello there," I said. "I'm glad to see you're well."

Frankie looked up to see who I was talking to. A large black raven with sleek feathers and a notch on the left side of her beak called down to us and even mimicked a "Hello there," throwing my voice back at me in the way these smart, playful birds some-times did.

"A friend of yours?" the newspaper editor asked.

I nodded.

"I named her Varella. Come out here once a week to feed her, even talk about life. When I first moved to Portland, I didn't know anybody. And the prospect of making friends was a little overwhelm-ing. So imagine my surprise when I came here to explore the faerie houses, and this beautiful bird kept me company, even letting me hand feed her."

"Varella? That's kind of a strange name. Why did you pick that one?" Frankie asked, putting her hands in her pockets to warm them.

Shrugging, I pulled out another bag of sunflower seeds and emptied them into my hand. But the raven did not come out of the tree like she normally did to perch on my wrist. We'd secured a good bond, and I loved her company over the last few years. But today she seemed a bit skittish, hopping on the tree's branches while looking down at us and occasionally swiveling her head from side to side.

"I don't think she trusts you," I giggled, piling the sunflower seeds on the ground at the base of the tree. "We should probably go. It's getting late. It was nice to see you again, Varella. And I'm sorry about my friend. I'm still teaching her about respecting other beings she may not understand."

We started to leave, and Frankie turned to me and asked, "Do you think I offended her?"

I shrugged.

"Ravens are smart creatures. They can solve puzzles and remember faces, even teach offspring to hate or trust certain people. Don't worry. I left extra sunflower seeds to make up for your comment," I said with a chuckle.

Frankie Dee let out a sigh of relief. I couldn't tell if it was genuine or not.

"Well, thanks," she said. "I wouldn't want the local raven community to seek vengeance on me. I live closer to Mackworth than you do."

We got back to the parking lot a few minutes later, and I looked at Frankie as the last few rays of today's sunlight washed over her bright blonde hair. As I stared into her chestnut eyes, all I wanted to do was take her home and curl up on the couch together, watching a movie.

Instead, I said, "C'mon. Let's go get something to eat."

Frankie raised an eyebrow.

"I've got you figured out, FeeDee. If we part now, you'll probably try to sneak back to the office and squeeze in a few more hours of work, getting a sad 'dinner' from the breakroom vending machine or skipping it altogether. Or I could pester you to come with me, and we could hit up a little burrito place I like over by the Westing Hotel," I said.

The newspaper editor rubbed her arm while thinking this over.

"Why do you do that?" she asked quietly.

"Do what?"

"Try to. . . take care of me all the time?"

And suddenly we'd left the witchcraft lesson behind and moved into a conversation of dangerous proportions. A man in a leather jacket walked past us and climbed into his pickup truck, pulling out of the lot and driving across the narrow bridge that connected Mackworth Island to Route 1.

"Because friends look out for each other?" I offered.

"Friends?" she asked, and the question suddenly felt like a fence being posted in front of the gate to Frankie's heart. I didn't like that, but I wanted to respect her boundaries.

"Colleagues," I offered instead.

She cocked her head to the side.

"I don't like that word anymore," the newspaper editor whispered, rubbing her arm a little harder now.

I could do nothing but wait while Frankie worked out what she wanted to say next.

And then the fence came down entirely as she said, "I think I like pals better."

It was almost a whisper from her lips to my ears, and my gay little heart nearly came to a halt hearing her speak the words.

"Okay, Frankie. Pals," I said.

She nodded, scratching her chin again. And as we left the island of faerie houses behind, my brain, perhaps a little inappropriately, thought, *gals being pals.*

9

(Frankie)

As I drove Dad's old green pickup truck down Congress Street toward the doctor's office, my mind ran through the last week. Dawn had been in the newsroom every day, writing astrology columns, working with our page layout staff to design horoscopes, and pestering me to take proper meal breaks.

The witch was quickly becoming a regular presence in my life, and I didn't intend for that to happen when I hired her.

I didn't intend for a lot of things to happen, I thought, picturing how she looked in the parking lot on Mackworth Island, the evening breeze blowing her curly hair around her face like a blanket of surprises. That's what spending time with Dawn felt like. . . constant surprises. I was surprised at how much better I ate when she was around, surprised at how much more raucous the staff seemed in the newsroom when she was around, and surprised at how much happier I was when she was around.

"Earth to FeeDee! Did you hear me?"

Dad's voice brought me back to the present as he poked my shoulder. And the man had a poke that would break Facebook (haha, remember when that was a thing?).

"Sorry, yeah. What? You were saying something about. . . baseball?" I guessed, flinching as my fingers tightened around the steering wheel. Dad rock played quietly from the stereo I thought I'd muted a few minutes ago. Styx, I think?

Franky Jr. chuckled.

"I could tell you were lost in a thoughtstorm—"

"Brainstorm," I corrected him.

"Brainstorm," he said, rolling his eyes. "Anyway, no. Good guess. But I wasn't asking you about baseball. I got a text from your mother. She asked us to pick up some ground turkey on the way home after the appointment."

Sighing, I nodded.

"Right. Sure. Ground turkey it is."

My father put his arms behind the chair and stretched while grumbling. His Boston Blue Sox sweater wrinkled so I couldn't see Wallie the Blue Monster's face. The mascot was usually plastered front and center on Dad's baseball shirts and sweaters. He loved that weird blue creature with the orange hair.

"I can't believe your mother has us grabbing

turkey again. I can taste the difference, you know? Between that and beef? It's not nearly as sweet or crumbly," Dad said. "And the whole wheat pasta! What a sin. I have to confess to Father Carlos every meal I eat now."

I giggled and rolled my eyes. We drove past the divided highway-ish road that was Franklin Street. It cut Portland's peninsula in two, separating the Old Port from the houses and parks of Munjoy Hill.

"Quit your bellyaching, Dad. You still get to eat pasta. And the leaner meat and added fiber are better for your heart. For fuck's sake. It's been a year since your trip to the ER, and you're still griping about the food. Give it a rest, old man," I said.

Calling him "old man" usually shut him up as he spent most of his energy over the next two minutes just pouting and glaring at me while mumbling curses in Italian.

I suppose I should be grateful that he didn't complain about having to go to the gym regularly or how his bruschetta tasted different now. A worried daughter had to pick her battles. And at 30, I had more battles than I expected in life, trying not to think about the paper for once.

Come on, brain. I thought. *You need to be fully present for Dad's one-year checkup.*

"Okay," my brain said. "I won't think about the paper. How about scenes from the day Dad collapsed?"

Well, shit. Fuck you, brain, I thought.

Visions of the grizzled old newspaper editor clutching his chest and falling to his side swam behind my eyes. The sound of his panicked breathing and my cries as I yelled for Richard to call 911.

The silent and frantic promises I made God if he'd just save my father from whatever was trying to take him from me.

And who could forget the eternity I felt between Richard's short phone call and the paramedics rushing in with a stretcher, the questions they were asking me, and whatever gibberish I spit out in response?

Leaping into the back of that ambulance and holding my dad's hand tight while his eyes fluttered, and he grimaced. Tortuous hours standing outside an operating room offering God more frantic promises, some of which were still unfulfilled to this day.

"FeeDee?" his voice called me back to the present again. "Did you hear me?"

I nodded, wiping a small tear away from my left eye before he could see it. That time I'd caught the tail end of his words.

"Probably about half an hour, not counting however long we'll have to wait in Dr. Mendoza's office."

The newspaper publisher shook his head and rubbed his clean-shaven face.

"Uffa," he muttered. "Doctors. You schedule the appointment, you arrive on time, and they STILL make you wait half an hour."

My hand left the gear shift long enough to take his palm in my grasp.

"Hey, it'll be fine. We've got plenty of time," I said, my brain realizing the multiple meanings of that sentence as I tried not to cry again.

We drove past Remys department store, and I watched a cyclist nearly collide with a sports car as he tried to ignore the red light and zip through like the traffic laws didn't apply to him.

You would have been splatted like a bug, I thought as we continued past the art college and on toward the cardiologist's office.

"What do you think she'll say?" Dad asked, suddenly.

I shrugged.

"Probably not much. I imagine she'll tell you to cut back on dairy. Ask you how many hours you spend in the gym each week. That kind of stuff."

Franky Jr. grunted and crossed his arms.

"And if you aren't honest with the doctor, I'll rat you out and tell her you're still in the newspaper office five days a week!" I said, sounding more like my mother than I intended.

The man visibly flinched and immediately softened his tone.

"Oh, come on, FeeDee. I'm only in the office

for a few hours. It's practically part-time work being the publisher."

While we stopped at a red light outside of Channel 7's downtown TV station, I squinted at my father.

"You still need to watch how much you're working. I mean it. You're not allowed to overdo it in the office. That means going home when you're tired or not coming in at all if you're sick. Don't push yourself too hard, or I'll push Dr. Mendoza to write you a note banning you from the office for six months."

Dad's face paled as he threw up his hands.

"Alright already. I'll shave a few more hours off each week. Geez. Who raised you to be such a newsroom general?"

Smiling and feeling my heart warm just before the light turned green, I turned to the grizzled newspaper veteran with a small smile and softly said, "You did, Dad."

A few minutes later, we were seated and checked into the Maine Cardiology Clinic. Dad had to fill out his insurance forms again because he was on Medicare now. He grumbled about that, too, clicking his pen a few times in frustration.

The room was chilly and filled with several chairs that lacked cushions. A basic white tile floor squeaked depending on where you stepped. A large 125-gallon fish tank filled with an assortment of tropical plants and fish absorbed my attention. I watched clownfish, cardinalfish, and royal gramma swim around their tank with the ease of a Windows 98 screensaver.

All the while, my father continued to grunt and rub his temples trying to recall information for the medical forms. At one point, he even texted Mom.

We were the only people in the waiting area aside from a grandpa and his grandson doing one of those *I Spy* books together.

You're missing the fish, bub! I thought, not understanding how a kid would prefer to be looking for a magnifying glass or an orange shoe on a table of clutter.

"Eh, whatever," I muttered, watching one of the clownfish dart toward a toy pirate ship at the bottom of the tank.

When Dad came back from the receptionist, and I heard the sliding glass door clatter shut, I looked up and flashed him a smile. He did that boomer guy groan and sighed as he sat down in the chair next to me. I rolled my eyes.

He leaned forward and clasped his hands together.

"So. . . you see the report I sent you this morning?"

My heart sank as I recalled the glum spreadsheet he'd sent me. The Lighthouse-Journal numbers weren't great.

"Print ad revenue down 17 percent. Subscriber counts down nine percent. Digital ad revenue is up two percent, but it's a bucket compared to an ocean of declining print ad money," he said.

He was right, of course. Digital ad sales weren't ever going to make up for what commercial print revenue was 30-40 years ago, the very things that allowed newspapers to staff a wide variety of beats from recipe editors to Washington correspondents to film and theatre critics. You'd have reporters at every fucking civic meeting from planning commit-tees to school boards to library oversight groups, and more.

Now, we were lucky to have a reporter at every Portland City Council meeting. And depending on the agenda, we might not.

"What do you think, sweetie? Should we recon-sider the offer from Aidan Global Capital? Because at this rate, we'll be lucky if the paper makes it another three years."

Dad's tone wasn't defeatist. He hated the idea of a New York equity firm buying what our family built as much as I did. Well. . . almost.

I clutched my fists in my lap.

With my shoulders hunched, I ran through the numbers again. The same figures I'd burned into my skull every night before bed. If our revenue decline continued, we'd have to make more cuts. In six months, we'd stop being a daily paper and cut the Monday edition. In 12 months, we'd cut Monday and Tuesday editions of the paper. In 18 months, I would have to downsize our staff again and maybe look at outsourcing things like page layout to a cheaper graphic design firm elsewhere in the country. I'd gotten quotes from places in Kentucky and Oklahoma where other newspapers had already made this difficult choice.

It was a nosedive that, if not improved soon, would see our paper decline in quality to the point that we'd have to take it out back and Old Yeller the bitch. That was preferable to Aiden Global Capital running the place. I'd seen the newspapers they'd bought and stripped to skeleton crews, starved the page counts, and diluted their articles with AP wire content.

For those motherfuckers, it's always about bleeding as much profit from the news rag as possible, I thought. *And when they just can't bleed anymore, they shutter the publication.*

That's how you got news deserts where communities didn't have reporters to tell them who would be on the ballot or what the city council decided at their meeting on Tuesday.

"I think. . . we need to have faith," I said, trying to pull out of my mental tailspin.

"In God saving our paper?"

Shrugging, I smiled.

"Perhaps. And maybe he'll do it through this plucky new Horoscope Editor we just hired. You saw her demographics. She doesn't just have a wide national audience, but a lot of listeners here in Portland as well. When they get wind of the new content she's producing for our paper, I have faith enough of them will subscribe to reverse our recent trends," I said.

Dad nodded and then rubbed his chin.

"I guess we'll see. I hope for all of our sakes the new girl can pull it off," he said. Then his grin grew cheesy. "And, hey, if she doesn't work out as a newspaper editor, maybe she'll work out as a girlfriend."

Coughing on my saliva like only a true cringe master was capable of, I leaned forward and gasped for air, sputtering in the most embarrassing display.

When I could speak again and stop feeling the phantom sensations of Dawn's fingers squeezing the back of my neck while we made out, I turned to Franky Jr., whose face was red with booming laughter.

The grandfather and grandson looked up from their book and stared at us with befuddled faces as I scowled.

"That's not even remotely funny," I hissed.

"You're right, FeeDee. It's not funny. . . it's hilarious!" he said before slapping his knee and throwing his head back in laughter again.

I crossed my arms.

"She's just a coworker," I muttered, feeling the memory of what I'd said to Dawn on the island rushing into my head with a shrieking voice calling, "LIAR!"

Dad nodded.

"A coworker you spent hours with on Macworth Island last week?"

"That's exactly it!" I snapped.

"Name one other coworker from the newsroom you would go hiking with," he said, cocking his head to the side.

I scrolled through the list of names on our payroll.

"Ghost," I said, confidently.

"Ghost wouldn't hike if every computer and cell phone on the planet spontaneously combusted. You wanna try again or just save me the time and admit —" My father was interrupted by a nurse walking into the waiting room and calling his name.

Saved by the medical staff, I thought.

I watched as my father was weighed, had blood drawn, heartrate monitored and listened to by three different devices, and finally a conversation with Dr. Mendoza, who looked over his numbers on her computer screen.

She sat on a red stool, legs crossed, long black hair pulled back into a ponytail. The doctor was around my age and looked like she'd just finished her certifications. But her brown eyes were full of confidence. The white coat covering her russet brown skin wrinkled a bit when she leaned forward to speak with my father.

"Well, Mr. Ricci, the numbers on my screen show a recovery that's roughly in line with someone who was on an operating room table a year ago.

Ms. Ricci tells me you've been exercising more and adjusting your diet as needed. That's promising, but why don't you tell me how you feel?"

Dad wasn't one to complain. But his doctor gave him a chance to ask questions. And she'd really listen to him. So, the inky wretch sighed and asked, "How long will it take for me to feel. . . not so tired again?"

Dr. Mendoza cocked her head to the side.

"Are you dealing with a lot of fatigue?"

He shrugged.

"Things just. . . seem to take a lot more out of me than they did before. And I'm not used to that. It's a little frustrating, to be honest. I figured six, eight, even 12 months later that feeling would fade, but it hasn't."

Looking back at the screen again before answering, Dr. Mendoza nodded.

"Well, Mr. Ricci, I think you're a patient with heart trouble recovering in your mid-60s. And while you've made adjustments to physical activity and diet, you might just have to accept the fact that age and the heart attack have slowed your pace. It's not uncommon for men in your demographic to feel this way even years after surgery."

My father didn't interrupt her.

"But I view this as a chance to reshift your priorities in life. You're still putting. . . what? Twelve to fifteen hours a week in at the newspaper? In addition to hitting the gym three or four days a week?

That's a decent load for a lot of people. If you're increasingly fatigued, maybe lighten your workload and replace it with a new hobby, something not as stressful. And if you still find yourself wanting more energy, I'm happy to refer you to a nutritionist who can help you figure out if different vitamins or further changes to your meals might help."

With a chuckle, my father leaned back on the patient bed.

"So, what you're telling me is. . . I'm getting old?"

Dr. Mendoza leaned a little closer and without even a hint of bashfulness in her voice said, "Franky, you've been old for years now. It ain't something new."

The room went silent. And then, in unison, my father and I slapped our knees and laughed until I'm sure the nurses outside were staring at our exam room door in confusion.

When we quieted down, Dr. Mendoza turned off her computer monitor and said, "But you know what? My father would say he's earned those years and that growing old is a privilege. Not everyone is granted that gift to walk so far along the path."

"Amen," my father said.

"Do you have any more questions?"

He shook his head.

"Then I'll look forward to seeing you in six months, Mr. Ricci. Think about what I said. You've worked hard all your life. And from looking at Ms. Ricci, I can tell you taught her the same thing. How's your health, by the way?" she asked, suddenly turning to me.

I shook my head, caught off guard by the shift in her attention.

After realizing I hadn't said anything, I finally spoke up, "All quiet on that front."

She raised an eyebrow and hid a smile.

"Heart conditions are sometimes passed down from parents to their kids. With your grandfather having died from a heart attack and your father nearly suffering the same fate, I'd just keep an eye on yourself, yeah? Since your father is a patient here, you can always schedule an appointment for an exam, and we'd get you booked fast."

I showed her my palms as I stood.

"I appreciate the offer. And I'll keep an eye on my ticker, bub. But for now, I've got nothing to report, Dr. Mendoza."

She nodded.

"I'll leave you both, then. You can schedule your next appointment at the front desk. Take care, Mr. Ricci. And you too," she said, winking at me. I fought a scowl.

Back in the pickup truck, I sighed.

"Something wrong, FeeDee?"

I started the vehicle, and the air kicked on with its usual old stale smell.

"I. . . want you to consider what the doctor said about cutting even more hours at the paper," I said.

Dad crossed his arms.

"Oh, I'm just a little tired here and there. It's not a big deal —" he said before I interrupted him.

"Please? I just. . . think about what happened to Grandpa. And what almost happened to you. It was really close, Dad."

I was fighting back tears while my father was fighting back an argument.

"If you won't listen to your cardiologist, you should listen to me. I'm your daughter, and I need you to take care of yourself for me because. . . I still need you. I always will."

Watching his face turn downward, I sighed again. For a minute, the truck engine was all we heard. The vehicle was old but still had a few miles left in it. And we needed every single one it could spare.

"Okay, FeeDee. Okay. I'll take Mondays off. Maybe I'll go fishing or something. Is that better?"

Nodding, I took his hand in mine.

"Thank you."

Another beat of silence.

"So. . . turkey?" he asked.

"Turkey," I said, and off we went to the store.

———————————————

10

(Dawn)

———————————————

Heat rose from the frying pan as the cooking oil I dropped in slowly spread around the stickproof steel surface. Outside, I heard Billie call out and then the Fates made a few noisy clucks before going silent.

I tossed a popcorn kernel into the pan and put a glass lid on top, waiting for it to pop. Checking my phone, I saw a text from Frankie Dee. But in my phone, she was listed under "Frankie (Pal, Not Colleague)."

She'd written, "On my way."

But because lesbians are terminally late for every event they attend, I assumed my pal sent that before even having her shoes on. In fact, the exact order of events was probably: send a text, watch a couple of videos on TikTok, remember the event, mad scramble for shoes and a jacket, and then leave the house.

With a quiet little POP, the dry kernel trans-formed into its yellow and white counterpart, the movie-watcher's favorite companion. I tossed it into my mouth, only burning my tongue slightly in the process. Then, I poured several more kernels into the hot, oily pan from a glass jar labeled, "Iowa Organic Popcorn."

These kernels came from a farm in Iowa owned by a butch lesbian couple. Our school took a field trip to their farm in 9th grade for the usual farm fun, a hay maze (or a maize maze, as I jokingly called it), a petting zoo, and crop science lessons.

All the other kids were fussing over the lambs or screaming and laughing from inside the maze. But I just wanted to learn more about the farmers who'd blown my mind. Women. . . can be together. Like — just be together, in love. That realization felt like something so simple and foundational I should've learned years earlier. But, of course, my Bible-thumping father and sheltered church-girl life ensured those kinds of "evils" were excluded from my purview.

Looking back, I'm not sure how he missed that we were visiting a farm run by two dykes. Then again, I guess that wasn't exactly advertised on the permission slip.

I just remember being glued to the hip of Sadie Henshaw all day long as she showed us tractors, different types of soil, and the feed for their animals. Her blonde hair was cut short and styled like any other man's hair in Linn County. She was a shorter, stout woman who never went a day without overalls and a ball cap. Her wife, Daniela, handled all of the finances and told us a little about things like farm subsidies and corporate farms vs. mom-and-mom operations.

Some kids left the cornfields that day wanting to be farmers. But I left wanting to be another girl's wife.

The sound of popping kernels brought me back to the present as I picked up the frying pan and shook it back and forth with the lid on.

A knock at my door revealed a certain news-paper editor had arrived safely. And as I poured the steaming popcorn into a large, blue Finding Nemo bowl, I called out, "It's unlocked. Come in!"

My mind played a brief scene of Frankie Dee walking into, not just mine, but *our* house and hanging her keys up on the keyring we'd bought while antiquing. She'd get home after a late night covering a library board meeting or some such, and I'd pull a chicken pot pie from the stove and — fuck. I had to stop this dangerous line of thinking.

She walked into the living room and took her shoes off, just as I was bringing in the giant bowl of popcorn.

"I brought a bottle of wine. I hope that's okay," she said.

I smiled.

"That's perfect. I'll grab some glasses from the kitchen."

Frankie watched me scoop a handful of popcorn and place it on The Morrigan's altar. She raised an eyebrow.

"Does the goddess of war and prophecy enjoy a nice salty sacrifice now and then?"

I snorted and returned from the kitchen with a pair of stemless pink wine glasses.

"First, it's an offering, not a sacrifice. And second, popcorn has been around since 3600 BCE. You can't tell me she hasn't tried it and fallen in love," I said, plopping down on the couch.

Frankie sat down slower and made sure there was a cushion of space between us.

"Does Artemis not get popcorn?"

I shook my head.

"I only leave animal offerings from things I've hunted on her shrine."

"You hunt?"

Nodding, I motioned toward my bedroom.

"Keep a hunting rifle in the gun safe behind my closet door. I head up to camp a few times a year to hunt small things. Rabbits, turkeys, pheasant, sometimes squirrels if I want to make chili."

Frankie made an incredible laugh and leaned in closer.

"Squirrels for chili? Are you serious?"

"What's so funny about that?"

Her smile was bright enough to light up the

harbor, and I wanted so badly for her to guide my ship into her port. My heart rate kicked up as she teased me.

Wait a second, I thought. *Is she teasing ME? When did we switch places?*

"Where on earth did you grow up eating squirrel chili?" she asked, crossing her arms.

I stuffed my face with popcorn before answering.

"Iowa," I said.

She whistled. Was this the first time I'd heard Frankie Dee do that? Holy shit.

"Corn girl," she said. "And now you're here, using our phrases like, 'up to camp,' without an issue in the world."

"I'm sorry. Are people From Away not allowed to use any Mainerisms?" I asked, huffing and eating more popcorn.

Frankie reached over and grabbed a handful.

"It's cute is all," she said, closing her arms and throwing back the entire mouthful of popcorn.

I sat there blinking.

"Did you just call me cute?"

"Hard tellin' not knowin', bub. What's my witchy lesson for tonight? Why am I sitting on your sofa?" Frankie asked with a dodge only slightly less artful than Neo's.

Shaking my head, I rolled my eyes. I'd remember her words and circle back around to them later, long after the wine had been poured.

"Your lesson tonight, FeeDee, is to learn the difference between Hollywood's idea of witchcraft and the *actual* use of the craft."

"So. . . movie night?" she asked.

I nodded.

"Double-feature. We'll start with *The Craft* and finish with *Hocus Pocus*," I said, grabbing my remote and turning on the TV.

"Shit. We're going '90s tonight. I kind of feel like I should have brought over Capris Sun pouches instead of wine," Frankie said, pouring me a glass.

"Hey, the night is young. It may not be the '90s anymore. But just in case you're nostalgic, we have technological advances like apps that'll allow an underpaid delivery contractor to rush into Hennie's and grab us Capris Suns and maybe even Dunkaroos or Fruit Roll-Ups," I said, elbowing my guest. My pal. My crush. But most definitely not my colleague or girlfriend.

The movie started, and it seemed like half of the wine in my glass was gone before the opening credits finished. Silence filled the couch as I fought to keep my eyes on the TV and not on the beautiful blonde bombshell next to me.

"Holy shit! Is that Neve Campbell?"

"Yes!" I said. "Just seven short months before two guys forever ruined her life with knives, a cheap voice changer, and a ghost mask. That was a great year for the Scream Queen."

We sat in silence and watched Nancy, Bonnie,

and Rochelle meet Sarah Bailey and introduce her to their witchy ways of worshipping Manon.

"Didn't they make, like, a billion *Scream* movies?" Frankie asked, turning our conversation back to a different '90s film franchise.

"Yeah, and they're each amazing in their own way, adding layered commentary of horror movies through the decades. The last couple of movies even had lesbians in them."

Frankie just smiled and looked back at the TV.

"She was my first crush, you know?" I said.

The newspaper editor turned back to me with a sloppy smile that made me want her lips on mine all the more.

"Who was yours?" I asked.

She snorted but didn't answer, trying to turn back and watch the movie. But I curled my legs up on the couch and smacked her toes lightly with mine.

"Hey! I asked you a very important question, FeeDee. You can't just ignore it. Come on. Who was your first celebrity crush?"

Scratching the back of her head, Frankie finished her glass of wine and poured herself another. Meanwhile, I was starting to feel my first glass kick in as a warmth slowly washed over me. For good measure, I poked her toes with my feet again.

"I'm still waiting," I mumbled.

The look she flashed me was hungry for just a

moment, and I felt my body tense. I know I wanted to eat more than just popcorn tonight. But did she?

As her cheeks burned, Frankie Dee blurted out, "It was Cassandra Peterson, okay?"

Neither of us was paying attention to the movie anymore as my smile grew wide enough that I could have turned toward the camera with an excited look on my face, that is. . . if my life was the mockumentary I sometimes imagined it to be.

"Elvira?!" I almost screamed. "Mistress of the Dark?"

Frankie rolled her eyes again.

"There's no need to get overexcited," she mumbled, crossing her arms.

I scooted a little closer. Three-quarters of a cushion now separated us.

"You're right. I guess there's not. It's just. . . unlike my first crush, yours actually turned out to be a fellow member of the Sappho Syndicate," I said, finishing my glass of wine and batting my eyelashes at Frankie.

Why are you acting like this? I thought.

That earned me a belly laugh from my movie date.

"Sappho Syndicate? Is that an actual organization you can join?" she asked in between laughs, doubling over almost in tears.

"Sure is," I said, feeling more of that wine seep into my brain (because that's how alcohol works). "We meet on Tuesdays in our matching plaid button-downs and hash out the latest edition of The Gay Agenda. Then, when business is done, we all do laps in the parking lot in our Subarus while blasting Chappel Roan."

Frankie finally stopped laughing and wiped the tears from her eyes.

We went back to watching the movie as I explained to my date exactly what we'd missed, about how the girls each cast a spell to get revenge or improve their lives. And right around the time Nancy's stepfather died, I realized that Frankie had moved closer to me. Only half a cushion separated us now.

Did she do that on purpose? I thought, sipping my wine. *No. It's only an inch or two. If she really wanted to sit closer, she obviously would.*

Unless. . . she was playing a game? No. Frankie Dee wasn't the type of woman to play games. I tried to focus on the movie again.

But my mind thought, *Which is exactly what would make her suddenly choosing to play a game so surprising!*

Shit. We gays really did tend to overthink and analyze everything to death, didn't we?

Show me a homo, and I'll show you an inflated sense of anxiety and a catalog of thoughts like "Was that on purpose?" and "What exactly did she mean when she said that?"

The rest of the movie passed by uneventfully. I even managed to quiet my brain long enough to enjoy seeing Sarah overcome the coven that turned on her.

"That was kind of fun in a B-movie cult classic kind of way," Frankie said, starting her third glass of wine.

"Yeah. It's always fun to revisit, even if a movie about empowering women through magic only goes so far when it's directed and written by men."

I got up to use the bathroom. When I came back, Frankie was checking her emails.

"Working during movie night?" I asked, raising an eyebrow.

She shrugged.

"I wanted to read Emma's transcribed interview with a woman running for Cumberland County Sheriff. But I can do that tomorrow."

"That's right, you can. Because you have more important things to worry about on date night like the Black Flame Candle being lit and resurrecting three evil witches."

I waited for the newspaper editor to correct me over calling this "date night," but she just turned her attention back to the television.

She definitely heard me, I thought. *She was looking right at me. Why didn't Frankie say anything?*

Scanning her face for some kind of smile, I found none and relented, sitting back on the couch as we waited for the film to buffer.

"So. . . Iowa? What brought you to Maine?" Frankie asked in a tone I assumed to be her interview voice. Did all journalists have one of those to fill awkward silences or make easy conversation?

"Fleeing my nutjob church-obsessed father. No offense," I said, showing my palms and flashing a smile. Truth was, my view of Evangelicals was pretty grim due to my upbringing and the state of this nation over the last several years. But maybe, if I could allow her the space to do so, Frankie might just repair a microscopic piece of my faith in folks who shared her beliefs.

"Ayuh, that'll do it," she said and immediately dropped the subject.

Before an awkward silence could grow, the movie loaded, and our attention was immediately captured by Bette Midler, Sarah Jessica Parker, and Kathy Najimy.

"So. . . they're like — evil?" Frankie asked, finishing the popcorn.

Before I could answer, I realized something had changed when I'd gotten up to pee. Our thighs were touching!

Holy shit! I thought. *There's no cushion left between us!*

Electricity ran up and down my legs, as I racked my brain to figure out what I should do next.

She wants to play? I thought. *Fine. Let's play. I'll bet she gets flustered and scoots back over. FeeDee's more of a chicken than all three of the Fates combined.*

"Yeah," I said, slowly stretching and casually draping my legs over Frankie's. "But they're really silly. They drain the life from her and turn that dude into a cat. And then they're resurrected in the modern day. Hijinx ensue."

Where I expected Frankie to push my legs off her or at least scowl, she instead called my bluff by reaching behind her and pulling down a white fuzzy blanket I kept on the back of my couch.

I blinked as she spread the blanket over us. Warmth continued to shoot through me, half driven by the wine, half driven by the pretty girl who just blanketed us. Under the blanket, Frankie settled her hand against my thigh, and I fought hard to keep from asking, "Who are you, and what have you done with my FeeDee?!"

Except she wasn't my FeeDee. She was just Frankie. . . my pal, my home-girl, my rotten soldier. She's my sweet cheese, my good-time gal. Right?

Okay. Maybe she's leveled up her game, I thought. *Gone is the sheepish coworker. Round two.*

I had one more move that was sure to tip the scales my way.

I scooted my shoulder closer, leaned into her, nuzzled my cheek against her neck, and left my head resting there.

Game. Set. Match, I thought.

And to my utter consternation, she leaned her head on top of mine, and the smell of her peach lotion was all I could focus on.

Frankie Dee was suddenly a new class of opponent. This would require lots of analysis and over-thinking. But fuck me. . . I was just so tired.

I took in another deep breath of Frankie's lotion and felt my eyelids slowly drop just as Max, Dani, and Allison wandered into the Sanderson cottage.

The last thing I heard before everything went black was Frankie's snoring. At least — that's what I assumed the noise was. It was powerful enough that if Paul Bunyan were still around, he'd wonder who was sawing through trees so quickly.

MORNING LIGHT STREAMED in through my living room windows. The autoplay on whatever streaming service we'd used last night (there are like a billion now) had eventually settled on a cartoon about a family of four blue dogs.

Not long after I woke up, I heard Frankie's breathing change, and she lifted her head from mine and turned to look at me.

A crick in my neck must have grown through the night because a flashing pain stretched from my shoulder up to my jawline. But I didn't seem to care as I turned to look into Frankie's honeyed brown eyes. She said nothing, not entirely awake yet.

My phone told me it was 9:17 a.m.

Before I could think better of it, I said, "At least this time you fell asleep on top of me."

The newspaper editor groaned and mumbled,

"Oh, shut up. I should have been at work hours ago."

We stood and stretched. I couldn't stop smiling while thinking about last night.

"Sorry we missed the rest of the movie," Frankie said, clicking her tongue behind her teeth.

I shrugged.

"Eh, it's not as good as *The Craft*. That's why I had us watch it last. You want coffee first or a shower?"

The newspaper editor rubbed her face and stretched her eyes wide open.

"Coffee would be divine," she mumbled before surrendering to my suggestion and stumbling into the kitchen.

I followed behind her with an inescapable smile. Closing my eyes, I muttered, "Blessed be."

11

(Frankie)

Dawn's Subaru had a new jasmine scent courtesy of some air fresheners she'd clipped to her middle air vents. My eyes lazily drifted toward the window as we entered the Old Port. A few clouds overlooked the hundreds of tourists milling about.

We drove by the Ocean Gateway, morning sunlight reflecting off the harbor. That was Dawn's favorite word to hear me say. She grinned anytime I said it. "Habbah," she'd tease, as I rolled my eyes.

A massive white cruise ship rested at the docks, having brought a few thousand passengers to Portland from god knows where. They'd start showing up in the last half of May, sporadically through the summer, and finally arrive in full force in early fall, just before winter hit and made everything colder than a witch's tit.

Inappropriate thoughts about a certain witch's

tits sitting beside me bubbled to the surface, and I cleared my throat.

I followed that up with a yawn and shook my head back and forth. Dawn giggled and handed me a Moonbucks coffee I hadn't even noticed sitting in the console.

"You know me so well," I sighed in relief, taking a sip of lavender oat milk latte.

"You're pretty regimented," Dawn said. "It's not hard to learn your patterns."

I looked her over. The black blouse and dark pants gave her a more "business casual meets witchy" look. She'd even toned down her eyeshadow.

"Is that what you've been doing in between writing astrology columns? Learning my patterns?" I asked, raising an eyebrow.

Dawn winked.

"I've been studying you from every angle these last few weeks," she said.

Heat flooded my cheeks, and I almost choked on my coffee. Sensing she should move on, the witch mercifully changed topics.

"So, why are we going to this conference again when you're clearly exhausted after staying up until 2 a.m. looking over. . .," her voice trailed off, waiting for me to finish.

"An investigative piece on leaking pipes in the West End," I completed her sentence.

Sighing, I stifled another yawn and prayed

desperately to God that this caffeine would kick in soon.

"It's the New England Press Cooperative. They have an annual conference in Boston. Every newspaper editor from Burlington to Providence will be there," I said as we drove by a cargo ship entering the port with several red and brown steel containers. It blocked my view of the few sailboats in the water.

Commercial Street wove around the peninsula's eastern border passing through the Old Port. Dawn stopped so a few tourists wearing sunhats and carrying bags from the Unholy Donut could cross over to one of the wharfs.

I loved that our city had a working waterfront, and clearly, millions of other visitors who came here to eat in some of the most-awarded restaurants in the country did as well. Portland was an entirely different place in May and June than it was in January. And it would only get more packed as we approached July and August.

"I thought you said the Lighthouse-Journal hadn't gone to the conference in a few years," Dawn said.

"We haven't. Budget shortfalls mean conferences are typically the first thing to get axed for newspaper staff. But this year is different. I'm actually an invited guest."

Dawn's head turned toward me so fast I was worried she'd need a chiropractor.

"You're a guest speaker? That's so cool! What are you going to talk about?"

I smiled and twirled my index finger around my ponytail. For some reason, I was having trouble meeting the witch's excited eyes.

"Not quite a guest speaker. The conference organizers just asked me a few months ago if I'd be willing to join a panel of family-owned newspapers in the region. There aren't many of us left, and go figure, they want me and two other editors from Vermont and Connecticut to discuss the challenges of keeping a newspaper in the family given ongoing media disruption."

I probably sounded like I'd read that straight from a pamphlet, but when I finally glanced over at Dawn, she was all smiles. Was she. . . actually impressed? Or was this just a polite act from a woman who had tried on multiple occasions to get into my pants? A woman who would have succeeded if I could get more than three goddamn hours of sleep at night.

Her green eyes were lit with what seemed like honest-to-god enthusiasm for my craft.

"Anyway, they're paying for my room and meals. Plus, I can meet folks who are in charge of press grants our paper desperately needs and hopefully leave a good impression."

We drove past several piers, including the entrance to DeMillo's, a large parking lot that led out to a boat restaurant people flocked to every year. No Mainer I'd ever spoken to frequented the place, but folks From Away just had to eat there.

If you want to pay $35 for a lobster roll, that's your God-given right, I thought. *Welcome to Vacationland, bub. Enjoy your $400-a-night Airbnb that took an affordable housing unit off the market.*

"Well, I'll be sure to attend your panel tonight. There's also one tomorrow morning I'm interested in on keeping comic strips alive in 2024," Dawn said.

We left the Old Port, and it wasn't long before a worn brown and white two-story diner came into view with its aged exterior. A set of stairs led up the right side of the restaurant.

"Ah, Becca's. You don't look a day over 30," I smiled.

Visitors often viewed the diner as the quintessential restaurant where lobstermen ate breakfast or lunch, coming ashore after an early morning of backbreaking work. Some still ate there, and I never had any issues with the place. Its reputation as a Portland staple was powerful enough that Gov. Janice Mylls ate breakfast there the morning after winning her reelection in 2022.

The diner sat wedged between a few industrial spaces with their own piers and docks. Then, just as soon as we spotted it, the restaurant was gone.

"I've never actually eaten there. Is it good?" Dawn asked.

I shrugged.

"It's fine. I've never had a bad meal there. I do interviews there sometimes for stories. Folks are friendly enough. Becca's still retains some of its salt-of-the-Earth flavor that keeps so many people coming back."

Stretching and feeling a familiar pang in my chest, I grunted.

Sure wish that would stop, I thought, grimacing.

"Are you excited to learn about journalism from all the industry pros tonight and tomorrow?" I asked.

"Strangely enough, I am. I was actually emailing back and forth with a guy named Dorian Fletcher this week about the conference. He writes the horoscopes for a few newspapers in Rhode Island. I'm gonna see if he has any sage wisdom to share. Apparently, he's been syndicated for almost a decade now."

My heart fluttered in a good way for once as I tried not to stare too long at the witch. She was. . . learning about the most important thing in my life. Dawn Summers was spending her own money to travel to Boston and attend a conference just to get a better picture of what made me an inky wretch.

Rubbing my arm, I couldn't help but smile and look up at the Casco Bay Bridge as we drove under it. Butterflies in my stomach scattered to every inch of my abdomen as I realized I'd be spending an entire two days with my colleag— I mean pal.

An entire Friday and Saturday in Boston

together while I did my best to wait for these festering feelings to fade away in a "Mr. Stark. . . I don't feel so good," moment.

A few minutes later, the blue and white Amtrak logo came into view as we pulled into the Portland Transporation Hub. Every time I came to this place, I couldn't help but think, *Shit. They really tore down a beautiful and historic train station for this awful location?*

We grabbed our bags and walked inside a carpeted room with a long wooden counter that served as the ticket desk. Behind the transportation hub, a handful of busses docked and waited for passengers. Next to the busses stood a rail line where the Downeaster train would pull into the station.

Five times a day the train ran between Brunswick and Boston. We were all set to board the 11:48 a.m. locomotive.

"I can't believe you've never ridden the train before," I said, sitting down in a row of metal seats by the Downeaster platform exit.

Behind us, a family of seven waited to board a coach bus that would take them to Logan Airport.

"What can I say? I grew up in Cedar Rapids. We didn't have Amtrak in our town. There's only one train, and it runs through the southern half of the state. The closest station was like an hour away," Dawn said, sitting down beside me. She leaned close, and our legs touched. When I raised an eyebrow at her, the witch looked in the opposite direction.

I see you, I thought, shortly before a shiver traveled from my thigh to my brain. *And I wish I could see more of you.*

My brain betrayed me with a few more thoughts before an announcer called for Downeaster passengers to board from platform C.

Dawn and I nodded to each other, stood, grabbed our bags, and walked down a long enclosed walkway where a conductor with a blue cap held the door open for us.

There, waiting on the rail for about 12 or 13 passengers, stood the Downeaster. A diesel locomotive followed by a cafe/business seating car, four coaches, and a rear locomotive. Another conductor stood by the train and directed passengers to business class or coach.

Dawn and I got in the rearmost coach as it was the least full and sat right in the middle, placing our bags on an oversized luggage rack above the seats.

"Wow. That was a lot easier than boarding a plane," Dawn said, reclining in her seat.

I just grinned.

"Told ya. Trains rock. Wicked easy to get on and off," I said.

It wasn't long before the train pulled away from the hub and started its southward journey to New England's biggest city.

After crossing the rail bridge over the Fore River, which was my favorite part because it almost looked like the train was hovering over the water, we clipped along at a good pace toward Old Orchard Beach.

The Downeaster raced by houses, across large fields, between patches of forest, and occasionally within sight of the coast.

Dawn checked her phone before turning to me and asking, "So, when was the last time you went to Boston?"

My heart skipped a beat as a woman's face rocketed into my memory. It'd been a trip not unlike this one about six months ago. I even sat in the aisle seat, just like then. But sitting beside me then was a marketing executive, not a witch.

The pain must have been obvious on my face because Dawn slowly took my hand.

"FeeDee?" she asked in a softer voice.

I shook my head, chasing away a single name I'd tried my best to burn out of every memory since then.

"Um. . . I went on a trip to the aquarium with my girlfriend at the time," I said, as more home videos started playing in my head of us holding hands and watching the harbor seals, walking past the jellyfish exhibits, and smiling at the penguins. "Margaret."

My heart skittered off the rails and crashed into a rock wall as her words echoed through my mind,

"I'm sorry, Frankie. That's just not what I want for us."

I blinked away tears as my ducts betrayed me in the worst possible way. I didn't want Dawn to see me crying over the former love of my life! Fuck.

Shitbiscuits, I thought, taking a shallow breath and willing my eyes to stop watering.

"I'm guessing I don't want to know what happened?" Dawn asked in a low voice.

Shaking my head, I cleared my throat again.

"There's not much to tell. We wanted different things. We went different ways," I said, looking outside as we crossed into New Hampshire.

An awkward silence filled our seats as, behind us, two men were debating whether a hotdog was a sandwich. If I hadn't been in such a dour mood, I would have turned around and recommended a YouTube chef who had a podcast about that very subject.

Dawn and I mostly fiddled around on our phones for the trip south.

A couple of hours later, we pulled into Boston North Station. A freight train had delayed us by about 20 minutes, which wasn't too bad all things considered.

Boston North Station was a huge block of a structure where Downeaster trains terminated. If you had a connection to any other Amtrak train like the Acela or the Lake Shore Limited, you had to hoof it to Boston South Station, a solid 20-minute walk. It wasn't fun with luggage in tow.

Several pigeons waddled and pecked at different parts of the room. A kiosk with drinks and snacks stood next to a cashier checking his phone.

Several exit gates stood on all different sides of us. I showed Dawn how to scan her Amtrak ticket and walk through the turnstile. It took her a few tries, and I tried not to giggle.

On the other side of the turnstiles stood a Sunken Donuts and a few other restaurants that bordered a sports memorabilia shop. Above Boston North Station stood a sports arena where their hockey and basketball teams played.

Dawn called us an Uber, and 20 minutes later, we walked into the Shilton Boston Park Plaza Hotel overlooking the Boston Common.

This hotel had hosted the conference for the last five years, though I'd only gotten to stay here once.

A marble pathway led up to the front desk, and I could already see a number of folks walking around with New England Press Conference badges. It depressed me the ratio of men to women I saw walking around with event lanyards, but that was newspapers for ya. At its peak or at its weakest, the industry would still be dominated by men.

And I'm proud to be pushing back against that, I thought. *Even if my newspaper might fold in three years if we don't boost our subscriptions.*

The clerk who greeted us wore a black jacket

that covered almost all of the ochre skin on his arms. A gold nametag sat pinned to his chest. "Bayani" was engraved on the nametag.

His black hair was cropped short, and he wore a million-dollar smile.

"Welcome to the Shilton Boston Park Plaza. Do you have a reservation?" he asked.

I gave him my name, showed my driver's license, and he typed a few keys on the computer.

"Okay, you're on the conference guest list, so I don't need a credit card from you for incidentals. You'll be in room 507, and the elevators are just around the corner. There's also a stairwell on the opposite side of the lobby if you need to get your steps in like I do," he said, flashing us another grin before tapping the Fitwit activity tracker on his wrist. It rested on a silver band.

Bayani had a tall, lean body, so, clearly, he got more steps in every day than I did.

"Did you have a reservation as well?" he asked, turning to Dawn.

"Oh, no. I didn't have time to make one. I'll just take whatever you have available," she said with all the carefree attitude that Dawn Summers carried with her everywhere.

To nobody's surprise, however, Bayani grimaced and said, "Oh, I'm so sorry, ma'am. All our rooms are booked for the conference this weekend."

The witch's face paled, and I wanted to shake her by the shoulders and ask, "What were you thinking?! Why didn't you book your room months in advance, put the details in two separate calendars (digital and paper), and then call this morning to reconfirm your reservation like a normal paranoid adult?"

Silence filled the front desk as Dawn froze.

I sighed.

"It's fine. She can stay in my room," I mumbled.

Dawn looked over at me with a face of apprehension.

"Oh, Frankie, you don't have to do that. I can really just find another hotel. I'll bet the Five Seasons across the street has spare rooms."

I crossed my arms and adjusted the bag on my shoulder.

"Really? Because I'll bet they're also booked full as that's the overflow hotel for people who made conference reservations but missed the cutoff to stay here," I said.

Like any adult with minor (and totally manageable) travel anxiety, I'd kept up to date with the conference's email newsletters reminding folks of deadlines to register.

Dawn's voice was caught in her throat.

I looked at Bayani.

"May I have a second keycard for her, please?"

He didn't hesitate.

"Yes ma'am," he said, working his magic on the machine and handing a plastic card to Dawn.

She took it shyly and followed me to the elevator after I thanked the clerk.

I wasn't upset. But I was flustered. My foot kept tapping. She was going to be staying in my room tonight? MY hotel room?!

What the fuck were you thinking? She could have tried one of the other hundreds of hotels in Boston, I thought, furiously.

But then that would have made meeting up for panels more difficult since she'd have to get a ride between here and wherever she ended up. And that'd just eat up more time going back and forth. This was easier. . . logistically. Yeah, that's right. This was about logistics. And absolutely nothing else.

I was sweating by the time we arrived at the fifth floor. Dawn hadn't said anything. We found room 507 easy enough next to a locked staff laundry facility.

Tapping my card on the sensor, a little green light flashed, and I heard a small clicking noise. Opening the door, we walked inside to find my biggest shock yet. The blood in my veins turned to ice despite the fact that I was sweating. Honestly, between the warm front and cold front meeting, a small tornado might form inside my body at any moment.

"Well, shit," I muttered. "They originally assigned me a room with two queen beds."

A thin black and gray patterned carpet covered

the floor everywhere except for the bathroom. A long wooden shelf supported a flat-screen TV playing a slideshow of Boston's skyline and playing soft instrumental music.

There, sitting against the wall next to a writing desk and a nightstand was a queen bed covered in a white comforter.

A quick phone call down to Bayani confirmed the worst. My room had been changed at the last second due to some unforeseen circumstances. And there weren't any travel cots available for us to borrow.

This is all The Morrigan's fault, I thought.

I wasn't sure she existed, but at this moment, the goddess was real enough for me to blame. I rubbed my temples while my heart tried desperately to find its normal rhythm again. But it failed spectacularly.

"You look like you're freaking out," Dawn said, crossing her arms. I still hadn't lowered my bag from my shoulder. Because the moment I put it on the ground, time would resume, and this would be our room for the night. OUR room. And OUR bed. Fuck me.

"I AM freaking out. Do you not see the dilemma here?"

"They. . . forgot to fill our ice tray?"

My voice suddenly took a shrill tone. I was almost screeching to the point only bats and billionaire orphans could hear me.

"There's only one bed!"

Dawn shrugged. Then a wicked grin overtook her lips.

"Oh, that's no big deal. When we go to sleep tonight, we'll both just shout, 'No homo!' in unison."

I scowled at her with all my might, and the witch, as usual, deflected it.

"What's the big deal? We've already slept together," she said, her smile somehow growing more devious.

I stomped my foot.

"That was an accident!"

Dawn put her hands on her hips.

"No, you falling asleep before I fucked you silly was an accident. Us sleeping together during the movie was just a happy coincidence," she said.

I stood there stammering all the more, looking for some loophole, argument, or comeback. All had forsaken me. Perhaps if I'd gotten more than two hours of sleep last night I could've come up with something.

But instead, my face turned the shade of a tomato, and Dawn slowly took my bag, setting it gently on the bed.

In my head, I let out one final shriek. *FUCK!*

<hr>

12

(Dawn)

<hr>

Warm. The bed was warm. But that wasn't all. Something lying against me was warm, too. The fuck? My brain was slow to wake and took another five minutes to remember where I was.

Right, I thought. *Boston. Journalism conference. Hotel bed.*

I'd been too late to book a room, and Frankie Dee had selflessly offered to let me stay in hers, the little golden angel. My little golden angel. I mean — just a regular pal-shaped golden angel. This. . . friendship was getting difficult to manage. And perhaps what muddied boundaries the most was the adorable person with her arms wrapped around me!

That's what I felt. A woman who was a spitfire in everything except romance was resting on her side behind me, warm breath blowing against the back of my neck.

In what universe am I the little spoon? I thought, opening my eyes and raising an eyebrow.

Still, the fact that Frankie Dee had managed to, supposedly, in her sleep, overcome a pillow wall she constructed before bed was impressive. I couldn't even be mad.

And let's be honest. I'd been dreaming about her arms around me ever since we fell asleep watching movies on my sofa.

My bladder was suddenly knocking on the door, telling me to hightail it to the bathroom, but I didn't want to risk waking Frankie.

Fuck, I thought for the second time this morning.

Sunlight filtered in through the curtains of our hotel, and I could barely make out the alarm clock saying it was 7:02 a.m.

As my bladder continued to send nerve signals to my brain, the equivalent of a neighbor who knows you're home, and repeatedly rings the doorbell, I took deep breaths. I could endure this. How hard could it be to wait for Frankie to wake up?

But as each minute ticked by, and I failed to enjoy the comforting presence of my crush, my urinary system only grew in power and frustration. Finally, I was released.

Frankie's phone alarm sounded off at 7:15 a.m. on the dot. The newspaper editor stirred and groaned, blindly reaching behind her to silence the damn thing.

Only when she'd stopped the alarm and hovered over me did she stare quietly. I rolled over and found myself in her suspicious gaze. I noticed the pillow wall she'd constructed had been demolished faster than a kaiju crashing through the Coastal Wall in Sydney.

"Can I help you?" I asked, a wry grin working its way across my lips.

Frankie looked at the decimated pillow wall and back at me.

"Have some boundary issues in the night, did ya, bub?"

I scoffed.

"Excuse me! What's your working theory? That I scooted backward into your arms so quickly that the pillows fell away?"

Frankie rolled her eyes and started to get out of bed.

I threw back the covers and shot toward the bathroom before all 10 of her toes touched the carpet.

"Mine mine mine mine mine mine!" I shouted, running for my life.

An hour later, we were both showered and picking out clothes for the day when our room service arrived.

I'd ordered blueberry waffles with bacon, and the newspaper editor was treated to French toast, courtesy of her favorite witch and new snuggle buddy.

"It just doesn't make any sense. How would I deconstruct the wall in my sleep and scoot next to you without being aware?" Frankie asked.

I shrugged.

"Maybe because you're chronically sleep-deprived and exhausted. So when you actually get a chance to rest, your body slumbers like the dead," I offered, taking my plate into my lap and destroying that waffle.

"That's not a plausible explanation."

"Plausible deez nuts, FeeDee," I said, smirking.

The newspaper editor put her hands on her hips.

"Anyway. . . I really enjoyed your panel last night on the importance of preserving family-owned newspapers in a time when financial firms are snatching them up to bleed them dry," I said. "You raised a lot of good issues."

Frankie's face went through a spectrum of emotions from remembering something that seemed to frustrate her to surprise at being complimented to confused by my sudden transition.

"Did you really just say 'deez nuts' and then compliment my panel performance last night?"

"Witches, right? We're so unpredictable," I said, giggling like a five-year-old who would always reliably snicker when someone said "balls" or "nuts."

We finished our breakfast and did our makeup. The routine felt. . . normal, us standing together in front of the mirror and bright lights, applying primer, then concealer, then foundation, and setting powder. I added carmine lipstick and eyeliner, which Frankie chose to forego, getting an early start packing her suitcase.

What if. . . we woke up together on more mornings and did stuff like this? I thought. *Ate breakfast, picked our outfits, and did our makeup in front of the same mirror. That would be. . . nice.*

"You're staring," Frankie said, though not without a small grin.

"Am I? Shit. Sorry. I was lost in my head."

"What were you thinking about?"

I glanced over at the television and cleared my throat.

"So — what's on your agenda today?" I asked, packing my bags.

Thankfully, my new bedmate let that go.

"There's a presentation on modern solutions to old printing press part shortages I'm interested in. It should be over by 10:30 a.m."

I nodded.

"The panel on comic strips I wanted to attend ends at 10 a.m. What time is checkout?" I asked.

Frankie picked up a little pamphlet next to the phone, even though I knew she had the time memorized, and read for a moment.

"Looks like noon. So we can check out, head over to North Station, throw our bags into storage, and find a place to grab lunch. Our train back home leaves at 3:45 p.m."

I did at least remember what time the Downeaster left. But, my pal had to be organized and announce that organization to the world, so I just let FeeDee do her thing.

As a famous princess once said, "People get built different. We don't need to figure it out. We just need to respect it."

The princess had some good messages now and again, I thought. *Autocratic tendencies aside, I mean.*

THE COMIC STRIP presentation ended up being surprisingly humorless, but it was still neat to hear a recorded interview with Bill Watterson. That'd been a nice surprise.

With half an hour until Frankie's panel ended, I decided to wander outside for a bit. It was cloudy but warm and humid. The wind blew my black skirt here and there as I walked past a coffee shop, an insurance office, a Tallgreens drug store, and finally came to a little metaphysical shop called Luminescence.

Texting Frankie where I'd be, I went into the shop, which was filled with rows of crystals, incense, a rack of new-age spirituality books, multicolored candles, carefully polished animal bones, beads, and more.

The smell of sandalwood incense wafted everywhere I walked.

Stocking the bookshelf was a Black woman wearing overalls with one of the straps unfastened and hanging behind her. A necklace with a moth frozen in amber sat around her neck. Her curly hair was cut short and dyed blonde. The store owner's right fingers were covered in silver rings of different designs and sizes. A nametag on her overalls read, "Olivia."

"Can I help you find anything?" she asked in a cheerful tone.

I shook my head.

"I'm good. Just admiring your store. It's lovely," I said, looking at the ceiling tiles painted black and covered with dangling glass in the shape of stars.

Olivia wiped her forehead and closed the box of books she'd been shelving.

"Thanks. She's my baby. I've had this space for about 10 years now, and she's still running strong," Olivia said.

Smiling, I nodded and said, "Well, here's hoping this place runs another 10 years and beyond."

The store owner put her hands on her hips and grinned, revealing a silver tooth among her other pearly whites.

"Blessed be," she said. "If you decide you want help looking for anything, please let me know. Otherwise, I need to get these books shelved before my wife gets back from the bank."

I turned and found myself shopping among a bunch of carved multicolored glass figurines. Birds, knives, cats, clouds, and. . . something I decided I needed immediately.

Among the glass figures stood one draped in a soft pink hue. My eyes traced its double wishbone shape. Someone had shaped a tiny clit that could fit in the palm of my hand. And I knew immediately that I needed this.

Giggling, I picked it up and took it to the register, right as Olivia finished with her books.

And a grand total of $15 later, I exited the shop with my purchase wrapped carefully in paper and stuck in my purse.

Frankie will get a kick out of this, I thought.

But everything in my mind came to a screeching halt when I took two steps out of Luminescence and spotted a bearded face I hadn't seen in more than a decade.

"Hello, Dawn," my father said, and every ounce of blood in my veins immediately turned to ice. The breath I'd been in the middle of taking caught in my throat, and it took everything I had to keep from coughing — or screaming. Maybe both.

"You're looking. . . healthy," he said.

And while I knew he'd danced around to find that word, it was probably the worst selection he could've made. Because when I heard the word "healthy," I was reminded of who I'd lost, who he'd taken from me.

I flinched, and he didn't seem to notice or care. Hell, maybe that was exactly what he wanted to see.

"And you're looking. . . well. . . present," I said, searching for a word in the venom of my heart and pulling back at the last second.

The truth was, my father looked old. It'd been twelve years since I'd seen him last, but his face and hair made it appear more like 20 or 30 years. Most of the curly grey hair on top of his head had thinned. Regardless, he kept it trimmed, like poofy hair itself was a sin. His blue eyes, which used to be so filled with life and vitality, seemed to have faded, like a half-drained swimming pool.

The beard was new. Curly ashen hair covered most of his jaw. It was kept oiled and neat.

I didn't recognize the black and gray suit my father wore. It was newer, smaller. And I realized it was because he'd lost weight, maybe 50 pounds.

A dead wife and runaway daughter will do that to a man, I thought.

"How," I started before my voice trailed off.

"Did I know you were in Boston? Despite the deluge of blasphemous things on your social media, I kept wading through it all for some clue about where you'd ended up. And last week, you posted that you were going to be in Boston for a conference. A little time on the Google told me there was only one conference in Boston this weekend. And a few more searches told me this was the closest. . . witchcraft store," he said, looking past me at Luminescence. His eyes narrowed, and a frown creased his wrinkled face.

I shook my head.

"Why are you here?"

He took a step toward me, and my heart skipped a beat. I gasped, but he didn't retreat. Keeping me calm clearly wasn't his goal.

Micah Summers ignored my question and lowered his voice.

"What are you doing, dear? Witchcraft? Divination? Consorting with spirits? I raised you better," he said. "Your mother and I —"

"Don't," I started, interrupting him. "Talk about my mother. Don't lump her in with your bullshit."

That earned me another frown.

"Twelve years, and this is how you talk to your old man? Like a brute or a thug?"

That's how it always was with Micah, pastor of the Westfield Church of Christ. How you dressed. How you spoke. How you walked. None of it could show impropriety. How many years had I withered under his blistering scolding? As many as I could handle before she died.

"When I don't answer your phone calls, you're supposed to take the hint that I've cut you out of my life," I said.

My chest tightened, and I could feel my breathing hasten. The sidewalk around me was a blur except for the six-foot-two pastor standing in front of me. People walked around us, ignoring the drama in usual New England fashion.

"Even Massholes know how to mind their own business. It's one of their few redeeming qualities," Keyla told me once while we were hiking through Acadia. I remember smiling then. Some native Mainers could be a little prickly when it came to folks driving up from Massachusettes on the weekends.

Fortunately, beyond the all-encompassing "From Away" label I'd earned by not having ancestors on Captain George Popham's ship, Mainers didn't seem to have many opinions on Iowans. Hell, my own opinion on most Iowans was worse than my neighbors here.

My father shook his head.

"We're family, Dawn. And life's too short not to be around loved ones."

His voice felt like a noose being tied around my neck, and it took everything I had not to scream and run in the other direction. Maybe that was what I should have done. And as much as I wanted to, my legs felt like they'd been transformed into cinder blocks.

"Leave me alone," I managed to choke out before falling silent again. My chest tightened even more.

"That's not gonna happen. You're my daughter. I've spent the last 12 years of my life trying to find you, and you're going to hear what I have to say."

My vision went blurry. Oh. Those were tears. Fucking hell.

"I'm a grown-ass adult. You don't get to stalk and harass me when I make the choice to go no-contact."

He raised his voice.

"That's enough! I'm not going to stand here and let you speak to your father like that. The very first commandment I instilled in you was to honor your father and mother."

With a small whimper, I closed my eyes and said, "That was back when I had a mother to honor. . . before you took her from me."

Micah's eyes snapped wide open, and his face became rage incarnate.

"You're spouting the same nonsense now as you did when you were 16 which tells me you're the same hysterical little girl as you were back then. I've told you once, I've told you a thousand times, God called her home. She's with the angels now, not in any more pain. How can you possibly blame me for ___"

"Because you stopped her from getting treatment! She didn't have to die. The doctors said it was treatable. But you were convinced this was a test of faith for our entire family. Funny how you getting Lasik wasn't a test of faith. It was just when Momma got sick that it was suddenly a matter of belief and righteousness."

Micah took another step forward and clenched his fists.

"Do you really think I'm going to stand here

and be lectured on faith by a witch? You consort with demons and spirits. You have no right to criticize me when you walk the path of Satan."

"You no longer get to dictate my beliefs. I made that decision at the age of 16 when I left your ass behind."

And where I expected more rage to follow, I found only sadness in my father's face. He lowered his gaze to the sidewalk and shook his head.

"Please, dear, come home. We've both lost too much already. First your mother, then you ran away. Our church burned down a few years after that. We're still meeting in a barn waiting for a new home. And a couple of years back, I lost your grandparents after they got that Covid shot. I begged Ma and Pa not to, but the doctors tricked them into taking it. They were dead two months later."

No big loss there, I thought. *They might have been the only people I hated more than my father.*

Trying and failing to take a deep breath, I said, "Being an adult means I can make my own choices. I choose to live my own life apart from yours. And you need to respect that."

With shocking speed, Micah darted forward and grabbed my wrist.

"And being my daughter means I'm responsible for your soul, girl. Your eternal soul! I am your pastor and your dad. I'm taking you home so you can put all this evil behind you once and for all. And you need to respect that."

A tractor-trailer drove by us, the engine backfiring, a sound like a gunshot filling the street and sidewalk.

I flinched and started to struggle away from Micah's vice-like grip. He gritted his teeth and said, "Do you want to know what your mother's last words to me were? She made me promise to take care of you like she would have. Your mother wanted us to go on still being a family after she died. Are you really going to spit in the face of her final wishes?"

I froze, terror driving a knife right through the center of my belly and carving a straight line up into my heart. While I didn't know what Momma's last words to my father were, I knew all too well what she told me.

□══□

(TWELVE YEARS Ago)

A GIRL of 16 sat whimpering in a metal folding chair next to her mother's deathbed. Mary-Jane Summers was gasping for air now and again and sweating bullets. Her sheets were soaked, her skin pale. Most of her once-bushy brown hair had fallen out.

The teen held her unconscious mother's hand. Her heart quivered, and she sniffled for what must have been the 50th time that hour.

A ticking wall clock said that it was 6:30 p.m. on a Wednesday. The girl's father was behind the pulpit leading an evening devotional, as he did every week.

Dawn wiped a tear away with her good hand.

Without warning Mary-Jane bolted awake coughing with a violent seizure.

The little girl jumped and ran to grab a new wet rag from the bathroom. She ran it under cold water and brought it back to her mother, placing it on her forehead.

Weary eyes turned to the girl. Dawn wasn't sure if her mother actually saw her with what little was left of her faded green eyes.

"You're still here, my sweet thing?" the mother wheezed.

The girl nodded before choking out, "Yes. I'm here, Momma."

As more sweat ran down Mary-Jane's face, Dawn ran over to turn on the ceiling fan, knowing in a few minutes, her mother would likely complain about being cold and ask for it to be switched off.

With a building breeze in the room, some of the sheets from Mary-Jane's bed fluttered. They did little to hide her emaciated body. She was once strong enough to work the flowerbed of her garden. Now, she didn't even have the strength to walk to the toilet. But it didn't have to be this way, of course. That's what the teen was about to learn.

"Sweet child, come sit with me, please."

Dawn rushed back to her chair and took her mother's hand, the woman managing a loose grip around her daughter's fingers.

"Listen. I was wrong," she said before hacking again and knocking the rag from her forehead. Dawn wiped her cheeks and then put it back. It seemed such a small comfort at this point.

"Your father. . . I should never have let him scare me with all of his hellfire and damnation talk. My mother was right. I shouldn't have let him sway me."

Shaking her head, Dawn felt more tears building.

"Why are you saying this?" she whimpered.

Mary-Jane turned to her with an expression weighed down by buckets of regret. There were more words of remorse in that stare than any adult should ever say to a teenager. She coughed until her entire body rattled with weakness. But eventually, Dawn's mother found her words again.

"Because you need to know the kind of man he is. When we first got word from the doctors, it rattled us and shook our marriage to the core. There was a treatment available, but I let your father talk me into relying on faith and prayer alone. And now, as I lie here with precious hours remaining, he's out shouting into a microphone while I'm here robbing my daughter of what little childhood she has left."

The teen was nothing but tears now, burying her face in Mary-Jane's arms, crying.

"Don't say that. Please. God's gonna —"

Mary-Jane interrupted her daughter with a tight grip.

"God ain't gonna do shit. I'm sorry, baby girl. But your father robbed me of my life, and I'm left with nothing but pain and bitterness in my final hours. Oh, sweet girl, I'm so sorry to dump this on you. You deserve to be happy, and you won't be as long as that man is in charge of your life. He will use that holy book of his to beat you down just like he did to me. So, please, let me make one thing right before I go to be with your Grammie."

All Dawn wanted was to lie there and cry, but Mary-Jane ran her thumb across the teen's face and gently pushed her up.

"Listen close. Before midnight, I'll draw my last breath. This body has had it. Now, I haven't spoken to Freyja since I met your father. And with each waking moment that I lie here in agony, I wish I'd chosen to stand by the goddess my mother worshipped, the one I turned away from. But I'm begging her now, in my final hour, to get you to safety."

For a moment, Dawn couldn't tell if her mother was delirious or in prayer or giving her instructions.

Still, the teen wiped her face with her shirt and listened.

"Here's what will happen. Your father will be home around 9 p.m., and by then, you need to be gone. In the back of the cabinet above the stove, there's an old oatmeal tin. It should have enough money inside to get you somewhere far from this wretched home, the home I curse with my final breath. Buy a bus ticket. Buy five bus tickets. Just get somewhere safe. If Grammie were still alive, I'd send you to her. Instead, I have to trust you can think of someone to turn to. Can you picture them now? Someone you trust to help?"

The teen racked her brain, a swirling storm of grief and chaos. No 16-year-old should be given instructions like these. She closed her teary eyes, and two farmers came to mind. Their images floated to the forefront of her consciousness. They might be able to help her. Surely they'd understand her situation, right? A dead mother. A gay teenager running away from a religious household? Surely they'd help.

"You're thinking of someone?"

Dawn nodded.

"Momma, can't you just. . . please. I'm scared," the girl whispered.

"Oh, my sweet baby, I know. I'm scared too. I wish I could protect you from him. I wish I could carry you to safety with my own two arms. But I trusted the wrong man. I let him rob me of my strength and youth. And all I can leave you is a tin of cash I squirreled away through the last couple years. Oh — please turn the fan off. I'm shivering."

The teen got up and did as she was told. Then she was right back in that chair, holding her mother's weakening hand.

"Here's what you'll do. You'll sit here and cry with me for 10 minutes. I'll hold you. You'll get as much of it out of your system as you can. Then, you're going to give me a hug and go pack a suitcase. You'll take the money tin and find the people who will help you figure out where to go next. Okay? I'm so sorry, sweet baby. I'm sorry. This is all I can do for you. Now come here. Into my arms one last time."

"Momma!" the teen cried, flinging herself into the bed before doing exactly what her mother told her. She would eventually find her way back to that farm and a pair of sympathetic women who held her together long enough for Dawn to find out where she wanted to go.

But that was after the 10 minutes. The last 10 minutes of her childhood, where a baby girl got to whimper into her mother's arms and find whatever shred of comfort the matriarch and reborn witch had left to offer.

And that 10 minutes may have felt like an eternity to the crying girls holding one another in the bed. But later, when they both looked back on it, one in this life and one in the next, they'd both swear it wasn't long enough.

(PRESENT DAY)

I PULLED against my father's grip one more time, tears streaming down my face as I remembered that final 10 minutes. The last time I saw my Momma. And that goodbye only happened because of this man in front of me, a man I hated with all of my heart.

You don't forgive someone for taking your mother away. Not after 12 years. Not after 112 years.

"Momma's last wish was for me to be happy and away from you," I said.

Micah scowled and tightened his grip. I'd have a bruise on my wrist tomorrow, just one more way this man had hurt me.

"You don't look all that happy."

"I was until you showed up."

"When we get back to Cedar Rapids, I'll make sure to remind you what real happiness looks like."

I clenched my free hand into a fist. With her final words, Momma prayed to Freyja that I might escape this man. Through the years, I'd come to find good works and blessings from my own goddesses, as my grandmother and mother had before me.

"Time to go," Micah said before a familiar voice rang out behind him.

"I couldn't agree more," she said.

And I watched my father get yanked backward and tossed to the ground. He didn't bang his head, but his ass would be bruised for a week after it hit the concrete at that speed.

Standing in his place, gently pressing her fingers to my wrist and checking for bleeding or other injuries was a certain newspaper editor.

She looked at the tears lingering down my cheeks. After a gentle wipe of her thumb across my face, Frankie pulled me close, and I fell silent.

Micah looked up, nothing less than wrath in his face as he barked, "Who the hell are you?"

"I'm your daughter's employer. Did you know she's an accomplished writer for one of the largest newspapers in New England? Every day, my newspaper goes out to thousands of subscribers who have nothing but kind words for her articles."

"What does that have to do with —" Micah started before Frankie Dee cut him off.

"Sir, I wasn't finished speaking yet. I still had more bragging to do on your daughter's behalf. Did you know she built her own business from scratch? She took an idea and turned it into a successful product with a million listeners every single day. Dawn owns her own home. She works two jobs.

And she's the kindest, most accomplished woman I've ever met."

My father looked as shocked as I did as Frankie went on, and I felt warmth return to my heart at last. If my dad was a fire-breathing dragon trying to take me back to his lair and away from this sinful world, then Frankie stood with her heart blazing, sword drawn, and shield held high in my physical and emotional defense.

And gods help me, it was all I wanted in this moment.

"I say all that to finish with this: If I ever see you talking to Dawn again or god forbid laying a finger on her, I'll drop your body into my newspaper's printing press and watch as you're flattened by six tons of steel machinery. You got that, bub?"

We were both frozen in silence but for very different reasons. To Boston's credit, people continued to walk around us, ignoring the journalistic threat of a lifetime.

"C'mon, Dawn. Let's go home," Frankie said, offering her hand out to me. She represented everything I'd never had under my father's roof, first and foremost, choice. Everything about FeeDee was a choice. And in that moment, I made the decision to lace my fingers in hers as we walked away from a man I wished never to see again so long as I breathed.

And thanks to a certain newspaper editor, I'd probably get my wish.

13

(Frankie)

A shrill whistle pierced the foggy afternoon as the Downeaster charged north, leaving Haverhill. A tall man with a pronounced limp walked down the aisle past me. I only opened one eye to watch him move by me as he exited our cabin and continued toward the cafe car.

The train jostled our cabin, and another whistle called out from the locomotive.

A light rain trailed across the windows as the Downeaster traveled north toward the New Hampshire border.

Dawn and I hadn't said much to each other, her head on my shoulder. My cheek rested atop her frizzy hair.

We'd been caught in a mist walking toward North Station after leaving the human shitstain known as Micah Summers behind on the sidewalk. Dawn's father still hadn't risen from where I tossed him before we were out of sight. Leading Dawn away, I half-prayed that the ground would swallow that waste of human space. Surely our world had better uses for oxygen than to fill his lungs.

The leather seats we now rested in squeaked a little as our coach car rattled down the tracks.

But I closed my eyes and found myself lost in the sad bluesy tones of Dawn's music.

A single pair of white earbuds stretched between us so we could both listen to the witch's "Sad Girl Days Vol. 2" playlist. We each had one earpiece as quiet filled the rest of the car. Aside from an older woman reading a magazine in the seats closest to the bathrooms, we were the only ones in this section.

It was chilly, which wasn't all that unusual for the middle of May. Dawn shivered a little and scooted closer to me. And where before today I would have flinched and lightly scolded her, now I just lifted my head and fetched a light jacket from my duffel.

She opened one eye to watch as I unfolded the garment and wrapped it around her.

"Great, now I'm going to smell like peaches," Dawn mumbled.

"Does my lotion bother you that much?" I asked, resting my cheek on top of her head again. Without realizing it, I'd inhaled the smell of her champagne toast shampoo and conditioner. Normally, I'd have panicked upon noticing what I just did, but I was too tired. Rescuing my girlfriend (no — wait — I mean, pal) from her abusive father drained me.

"No. . . it's just hard to stay bummed and moody when I smell like fruit," Dawn said, opening both eyes now.

"Well, I'm sorry to ruin the vibe. Can't the melancholy singer dude put you back into a moody. . . mood?" I asked, stumbling for words. But definitely not because of proximity to a certain witch.

"I told you when we started this playlist that his name was Steve Conte. He plays guitar and sings with some different groups down in New York."

I closed my eyes again.

"Right. And what's this song called again?"

"Heaven's Not Enough," she said softly.

We closed our eyes and listened to Mr. Conte sing about. . . I dunno. I was always shit at deciphering lyrics. Something about the pain of leaving people behind? I had no clue.

The next track was a song called "Words That We Couldn't Say," followed by another named "Call Me Call Me."

I eventually got up to pee.

"You gonna be okay for a few minutes?"

Dawn nodded without opening her eyes. She grabbed my purse and placed it between the seat tops to lean her head against it after I wrestled my wallet out.

I guess the peach lotion doesn't bother her all that much after all, I thought, walking away, but saying nothing.

Sliding the bathroom door closed, I was shocked to find everything surprisingly clean. The floor wasn't even that wet.

Well shit, I thought. *How about that?*

As I washed my hands, I looked in the mirror, unsure of what I was searching for. Some answers to the many troubling questions my bothersome heart persisted in asking? Some surety about what I was doing with this woman sitting next to me? The solution to a riddle that would clear up any more misunderstandings between us? I couldn't say for sure.

But I settled for blowing my bangs out of my face and asking the girl in the mirror, "What are you doing?"

With little prompting, my mind answered back, "Comforting someone dear to me."

That lead to further questions like, "Can coworkers be dear to you?" And further answers like, "Pals can be dear to me," before I sighed and exited the restroom.

The older woman sat reading a magazine called *Amazing Aquariums.* She briefly glanced up at me as I almost dropped my wallet in her lap and performed an awkward dance to catch it at the last second.

"Sorry," I whispered.

She shrugged and went back to her reading.

I cleared my throat, and the older woman glanced up at me again.

"Do you know if the cafe car is forward or backward?" I asked.

Shrugging for a second time, she merely replied, "Hard tellin' not knowin', bub."

Frustrating as that might have been to anyone else From Away, it just reminded me I was in the presence of a Mainer. I grinned.

"I'd wager that I CAN get there from here."

My fellow passenger didn't respond to that, lowering her chin and resuming what must have been the most amazing article on aquarium cleaning and maintenance for tropical fish. But I did notice the edge of her lips curling upward.

I shivered, walking between train cars as the cold air washed over my shoulders, and a few drops of rain fell onto my head, getting lost in my ponytail.

Every table in the cafe car was filled with Amtrak employees. The conductors were talking or going over paperwork. I shrugged and ordered a couple of hot teas from a cute transfemme working the register.

Returning to my seat, I offered Dawn one of the teas.

"Thanks," she said.

I nodded, feeling the warmth through my paper cup. Steam rose from my tea and danced between

Dawn and me for a minute before drifting against the window's chill and fading from sight.

"What's this song called?" I asked, putting the earbud back in place.

"Midna's Lament."

"What the fuck is a Midna?" I asked, raising an eyebrow.

Dawn sighed.

"A sad little imp that breaks your heart."

I didn't follow that up with any more questions.

Without any prompt, Dawn told me a story after the Downeaster pulled away from the station in Exeter.

"I. . . ran away from home when I was 16," she started, before proceeding to tell me about her mom's illness and final hours. I quickly found more reasons to hate her father. But all of that paled in comparison with the wave of sadness that washed over my heart when I realized Dawn had been on her own since before I had my driver's license.

The sad truth was I tried to picture myself going through even half of what she did, and I knew I'd crumble. Kids weren't made to carry those kinds of burdens. They were made to run in the woods with sticks making forts. They were made to stay up late watching scary movies even though they'd be too scared to fall asleep. And they were made to ride their bikes through giant mud puddles to see who could make the biggest waves.

Without thinking, I slowly took Dawn's free

hand. Her eyes widened. Neither of us said anything for a moment as the music changed.

Finally, I broke the silence by saying, "Wow. . . this one's very techno."

"Courtesy of an outstanding Greek musician named Vangelis, one of the best composers of the '70s and '80s," Dawn whispered, staring at our hands. She rubbed her thumb over my knuckles, and I felt tiny shivers race up my elbow and graze my spine.

"Hey FeeDee?"

I turned to face the witch, whose eyes were just shy of tears. Dawn's eyes lingered just across the border from Tears in a tiny village called Somber.

"Will you tell me how your folks handled your coming out? I can only assume it went better than mine given that you still love them," she said. Bitterness trailed at the end of her sentence.

We arrived at Durham, and the University of Southern New Hampshire came into view, students passing in and out of the fog and mist. There was no escaping the overcast weather today.

I sighed, thinking back to those awkward conversations I had with my very Catholic parents. They never got mad or disappointed. It was just. . . stiff for a day or two around the house. And then, things seemed to get back on track for most of the family soon after that.

"Well, let's see. My little sister rolled her eyes and said, 'Duh.' My father's exact words were,

'Hey! I like women too.' And my mother didn't say anything for a few minutes, just tapping her finger against her cheek. But eventually, she smiled and gave me a hug. When I asked her what she was thinking about, Mom said, 'If the Pope isn't going to judge you, what right do I have? You're my daughter, and I love you.'"

Dawn took a sip of her tea and cleared her throat.

"I dunno why I thought hearing that story would make me feel better," the witch mumbled.

And my chest ached for her like never before. Tremors of sorrow split the ground of my heart, and I put my seat table down, setting my tea on top of it.

Pulling Dawn in close with both of my arms, I heard her stifle a small sob.

I alternated between kissing the top of Dawn's head and lightly stroking her hair. My need to comfort her overrode the part of my brain screaming, "What are you doing?!" In fact, I'm pretty sure the comfort portion of my brain pushed a button, activated a trap door, and caused the screaming piece to fall into a black abyss.

"If it helps you feel better, my uncle Lorenzo didn't handle my coming out well. He did all the things your father probably would've done if you'd stuck around. He left pamphlets for my father to read, sent me angry texts, and aggressively called every romantic partner I brought home my 'friend.'"

Dawn buried her face in my shoulder.

"I don't suppose he ever tried to drag you out of state?"

"He's never had to. Enzo lives up in The County. The worst he's done is make passive-aggressive comments to my father about letting me run the paper instead of him while Dad was still in the hospital."

The Downeaster didn't stop in Dover for some reason. Perhaps because there were no passengers scheduled to board or disembark there. And soon, we were crossing the border into Maine.

"Your uncle sounds like an asshole," Dawn said.

I snickered.

"He's not my favorite person in the world. And I still feel like shit whenever he's around because of how he talks to me and the girls I've dated. But our paths don't cross too often. Truth be told, I think Portland scares him with all the homes and businesses that hang rainbow flags in their windows."

I watched the old woman roll up her magazine and head toward the cafe car.

"Hey, FeeDee?" Dawn asked with a sudden vulnerability that surpassed anything I'd heard from her yet.

"Yeah?"

"Thanks for coming to get me," she said, so quiet that I almost didn't hear her.

I kissed her head again.

"I meant everything I said today, Summers, including my promise to run him through my printing press if I ever see him near you again."

The witch raised her head a little to stare at me.

"Did you just call me 'Summers'?"

"Got a problem with it? I was leaning toward Witch Bitch, but Summers was more convenient."

"How so?"

I giggled.

"Well, if I called you the other name, I'd have to mention it during confessional. It'd get tiresome," I said.

Dawn finished her tea and set the empty cup on the floor between her feet.

"You confess every time you say naughty words?" she snickered.

"Oh yes. Father Carlos is very cool with the gay thing, but he's surprisingly strict about using language. One time I called another kid an asshole on the playground behind our parish because he took my phone. The priest scolded both of us, him for stealing and me for cursing."

That earned me another laugh from Dawn.

The witch placed our united hands in her lap and ran her thumb over my knuckles again.

"You're very sweet, ya know? I wouldn't want anyone else to be my pal," Dawn said, closing her eyes and sighing.

The witch ran her nails lightly over my arm and

knuckles, skimming the surface of my skin, now covered in goose flesh.

I let out a quick huff and froze before slowly closing my eyes and surrendering to the shivers rushing up my arm like cars on Interstate 295 each summer.

With a strained tone, I managed to squeak out, "Thanks. You're not so bad yourself."

And if I wasn't on a moving train, I'd have exited the room with finger guns, shortly before realizing my humiliating error and self-immolating from embarrassment.

Since I couldn't do any of those things, I just kept my cheek on top of Dawn's head and listened to her music some more, waiting for our train to take us home.

14

(Dawn)

With my fingers flying over the keyboard of an old laptop that should have been replaced three years ago, I sighed and wrapped up my column on misapprehension of the Death tarot card.

"Death is a word we instinctually fear as living beings with ticking clocks, but things are not as they appear when this card is pulled from a tarot deck," I read aloud, going over the first paragraph again and tightening up a few later sentences.

After saving the article, I opened Illustrator and put the finishing touches on tomorrow's horoscope graphic I'd made. It wasn't anything complicated, just a box outlined with stars and separate spaces for all the Zodiac signs.

Half an hour later, I sent everything over to Emma, who was editing my stuff tonight. Leaning back in my chair, I felt my back pop in two places.

"Probably my cue to stretch," I mumbled,

standing up and leaning against the doorframe until every muscle in my arms and shoulders had been pulled just tight enough to make my vision hazy for a moment.

Billie the Kid bleated outside shortly before I heard a small thump against the privacy fence.

"That's it, little buddy. Keep up the headbutting practice, and you'll be putting any pachycephalosaurus in the neighborhood on high alert," I giggled.

It didn't take long for Emma to email me back with a few suggested changes I made quick work of. But at the bottom of the email was a question I didn't expect from our evening City Editor.

"Happy birthday! Are you going to do your wild partying this weekend? I always hate it when my birthday falls on a weeknight," she'd written.

A twinge of. . . something struck my heart. I was a little surprised she knew today was my birthday until I remembered the offhand comment I'd made during today's episode of Dawn's Divinations.

What was it I said? I thought. *That I had no big plans for tonight?*

That sounded right. A commenter on my livestream asked about my special day, and I must have fired off a remark before my brain could stop it. It was one of my more endearing qualities. Or so I hadn't been told.

Keyla and I had been planning a birthday dinner, but her mother had been hospitalized with pneumonia back home in Denver. I wished her well, and Keyla flew home to be with her for a couple of days. The doctors said Keyla's mom would be fine, but my bestie was still tight enough with her family that she'd drop everything to rush home if she heard a suspicious sneeze over the phone.

I wonder what having a loving family like that would be like, I thought, self-pity once again coming into the one-bedroom apartment of my mind and kicking its shoes off, collapsing onto the sofa.

Keyla was pretty much my only friend up here, and I didn't know if she'd be back by the weekend or up for rescheduling our dinner. And, sure, I had a pal I could text. But I still didn't know where our increasingly muddy boundary left us. Did pals cuddle and fall asleep together? Did having a pal include rescues from abusive parents? We'd hit some equilibrium that left me both excited and frustrated as hell.

Frankie Dee had seemingly stopped caring about lines drawn in the sand when she let me stroke her arm and bury my face in her shoulder and neck. But I also didn't feel like I had a strong enough bridge to pull her into a tight kiss without warning, the way I'd been dying to since our first night together.

Shrugging and groaning, I sent a short email back to Emma along the lines of, "You never know what Fate will deliver to your doorstep."

I'd decided to work from home today instead of

going into the newsroom so they wouldn't have to see me mope. A ding on my email revealed a final note from Emma, "That's true. You never know," she'd written with a winking emoji.

That was the great thing about being a witch. Sure, you got funny stares when you talked about things like crystals, energy, and retrograde. But people expected you to say weird shit. It was the perfect way to dodge any troublesome questions.

"Hey, how's your mom doing, Dawn?"

"Only the stars can reveal her fate."

And then, boom. The inquiry was over.

I was wondering where I'd get takeout from when the doorbell rang.

Checking the peephole, I nearly jumped and fell backward upon seeing my girl—pal—coworker—person standing on my doorstep.

What the fuck, Fate?! I thought, quickly glancing back at my Morrigan altar, as though her visage would be standing there with a wink before fading into the sunset rays filtering into my living room.

Clearing my throat and trying to slow my heartbeat, I opened the door.

"Frankie. . . aren't you supposed to be covering a Historic Preservation Board meeting right now?" I asked, my fingers twitching.

She shrugged and said, "Emma's watching the livestream and will write up a little blurb. The agenda was pretty barren tonight anyway. C'mon, we've gotta get ready."

The newspaper editor lightly nudged me aside and walked into my house.

"Ready for what?" I asked, spinning to watch her.

"For your birthday kidnapping," she said, without missing a beat. The smile on her face seemed to obliterate any worry I had over the aforementioned felony.

I slowly closed the door behind me as a grin crept over my face. Maybe it was ridiculous to hear FeeDee say those words, or maybe I was just so ridiculously happy to see her. I couldn't tell which.

"My birthday. . . kidnapping?" I asked with a laugh. "What all does that entail?"

"Well, when I heard that my pal had no birthday plans, I went home, grabbed a nice dress, and put together an ultimate birthday abduction itinerary. Now, come on. Let's get ready."

My heart had warmed at least 10,000 degrees, and suddenly the colors around me were much more vibrant. Had I taken an edible an hour ago, or was the girl of my dreams taking me out for a surprise birthday celebration?

"Oh. . . okay. Yeah! That sounds like fun. What's first on the agenda?"

"Dancing."

"Dancing?!" I stumbled around the corner to my bedroom.

"Hopefully you'll be a little more graceful than

that, but yes," Frankie said, stepping into my guest bathroom to get changed.

Opening my closet, a single question kept running through my mind. Is this really happening? Is the girl I'm crushing on kidnapping me on my birthday? Did THE Frankie Dee give up work plans to cheer me up tonight? I've never had this happen before.

I threw several dresses on the bed and settled on a navy wrap dress with narrow gold stitching around the belly. I tied my hair back into tiny space buns.

The dark eye shadow I settled on complemented my dress as I picked out a matching lip gloss. If FeeDee was abducting me, I'd make sure she was getting a glammed-up birthday girl to dream about.

Lacing up a pair of black chunky heels, I took a look at myself in the full-length mirror and adjusted the dress with a few pulls here and there.

Damn, Dawn. You sure do know how to go from depressed to best dressed, I thought, giggling.

Grabbing a body spray from my counter called Iced Lemon Pound Cake, I lightly sprayed and walked through the mist a few times before going out into the living room.

I'd apparently beaten Frankie Dee. She was still in the guest bathroom, and I could hear Fleetwood Mac playing from her phone.

Aw, she has makeup music, I thought. *That's so adorable.*

A few minutes later, my jaw dropped when a blonde bombshell of a woman stepped into my living room wearing a tight black sheath dress and a golden necklace with a butterfly charm front and center. She'd chosen to spend tonight dancing in red kitten heels.

Bold, I thought. *Very bold.*

This was one of the few times I'd seen FeeDee with her hair down. It hung loose across her shoulders as she looked me over.

"Damn, Dawn. You clean up pretty well for a surprise kidnapping," she said. Where did this unexpected confidence come from? This was not how I was used to seeing Frankie act around me. And, sure, it was a welcome surprise, but I also didn't know if this signified a new level of relaxed behavior that'd grown between us.

Was she. . . just finally comfortable being around me now? Had something happened in Boston that ripped out any stiffness in Frankie's behavior toward me? Or was I just reading too much into this? We gays tended to overthink things, after all.

"You look amazing," I said, eyes staring at her toned legs.

Frankie's eyes seemed to glaze over for a second, and she wobbled a little to the left before catching herself.

"Whoa, hey, are you good?" I asked as she shook her head.

"Yeah! Fine. Just didn't sleep well last night. Anyway, let's get this birthday dance train going," she said, grabbing my shoulders and pushing me toward our purses hanging by the front door.

I grabbed my Subaru keys, and we were on our way to a truly wild lounge called Bubby's.

The sun was threatening to sink further toward the horizon by the time I parked near the post office on Forest Avenue, right across from Bubby's.

"Prepare yourself, Summers. It's a lot," my pal said, with an uncharacteristic grin of mischief.

I nodded, and we walked into a world I did not expect to find in Portland. A chipped hardwood floor gave way to an honest-to-gods light-up disco dance floor, complete with Bee Gees playing over the loudspeakers.

Old lunchboxes hung from the ceiling, antique leather couches stood near well-worn wooden tables and chairs. Everywhere I looked, my eyes traced over small appliances and toys that belonged on "Antiques Roadshow."

A group of college kids were already on the dance floor doing their thing when FeeDee took my hand and led me over to one of the bars.

"What do you think?" she asked.

I blinked a few times, looking at the multicolored floor, before answering.

"Wild stuff," I said. "How old is this place?"

Frankie ordered us a couple of beers and handed one to me.

"This place is a Portland institution, been here since the '60s," my pal said as I took a drink.

We stood there watching more people dancing while we drank our beers, chatting about how summer was right around the corner and it was finally starting to get warmer outside.

"Almost June already? Geez. Have you read the next book club title yet? The one about the orc and succubus who open up a fantasy coffee shop?" I asked.

Frankie finished her beer and shook her head.

"No, I'm waiting for my audiobook credits to reset for the month," the newspaper editor said. "How's the one book you were reading? Something about space necromancers?"

I smirked, thinking back to the chapter I'd finished last night.

"It's. . . a lot. Like, the characters are amazing, and the worldbuilding is solid. But it's so bleak. And the story is so dense I get a headache. Sometimes I wanna stop. And other times I can't imagine my life without this series. It's a real roller coaster," I said, taking a final drink of my beer.

We set them on the bar, and I turned to FeeDee.

"Well, I believe you promised me some dancing," I said, feeling my stomach starting to do somersaults.

"Are you saying you're ready to cut a rug?" Frankie asked, placing her hands on her hips.

"Yeah, dame, right after we paint the town red," I said in my best old-timey radio announcer accent. "C'mon!"

We found our way onto the light-up floor away from some of the college kids. But more importantly, our bodies found each other.

Frankie froze for a moment, and I seized the opportunity to take the lead, something I expected she secretly enjoyed.

"Wham Bam Shang-A-Lang" played over the speakers as I pulled the newspaper editor close and rested my hands against her hips. Up close, I smelled her peach lotion. Memories of last week's trip to Boston and back spun through my mind faster than Leo's totem at the end of *Inception*.

The newspaper editor scooted even closer and took a breath. Her bare arms were driving me crazy, even more so than the stray strand of hair that drifted over from her face to tickle mine now and again.

We swayed with the music, and I was surprised to catch Frankie Dee's hips swirling against mine, moving even closer as we danced. It fanned the fire in my core as a storm surge of inappropriate thoughts washed over my mind.

There were things I wanted to do to this lady, had wanted to do to this lady, that I didn't know if she was ready for yet.

Sometimes I could almost swear by the look in her eyes that she wanted me to do them to her as well. Some thinning invisible line kept her in check, but I could feel it fraying every time we got together. And I wasn't sure if the thought of it finally snapping loose excited or terrified me. I didn't know how Frankie would react.

"What are you thinking about?" Frankie asked, cocking her head to the side.

"Just how pretty you look tonight," I blurted. Smooth.

Journey came over the sound system as "Separate Ways" filled the bar, and one of the college kids shouted, "My dad loves this song!"

I snorted before remembering I shouldn't be THAT judgmental. What was the witch motto again? "Do no harm, but take no shit."

Neither Frankie nor I were going to win any dance competitions, but I didn't think we looked awful. Nobody was pointing and laughing at us, anyway. But as the beer finally seemed to loosen my legs, I started to swing more from side to side.

My dance partner only grinned and spun here and there with all the motion of a creek after a rainstorm.

I laughed, which only seemed to spur her on more. Frankie Dee spun around behind me and threw her arms around my neck as we rocked to the beat. My core temperature MUST have been hot enough to roast a sirloin steak at this point as

FeeDee leaned in close and whispered, "Having fun, Birthday Girl?"

Spinning back to face her, I bared my teeth and said, "I'm having a blast. Are you keeping up okay?"

We danced for another couple of songs until the two of us were sweating and seconds away from what I assumed was running our tongues up and down each other's bodies. I intended to stay on the dance floor for Eurythmics' "Sweet Dreams," but seeing Frankie wince and grab her chest jolted me out of my reverie and back to reality.

Suddenly, the songs were just noise to further fuel my adrenaline as I steadied my dance partner, who was swaying again, and not to the beat.

"Hey! FeeDee, you good? You're starting to scare me."

She kept one hand over her heart and took a couple of slow breaths.

"It's nothing. Just tired. Can we sit down for a moment?" she asked.

"Yeah, sure. Let's go to that table over there."

I guided her, and now a few people were staring at us. But all I could focus on was her grunting and closed eyes.

"I'm fine. Really. Just need a minute," she choked out as I found my phone. She gently pushed it back down into my purse.

"No, really. I think. . . I just need some food. You want to grab some dinner?"

Quirking an eyebrow, I stared at my pal for a few more seconds until she raised both of her palms into the air.

"Seriously, all good. Just got a little dizzy is all. Just need some protein. Like you're always after me to eat regularly? That's all this is," she said.

I frowned, but she pushed on to another topic before I could ask her any more questions. This wasn't the first time I'd seen her do that.

"Hey, what do you want for dinner? My treat, birthday girl."

My stomach growled, which further loosened my attention span, and I cleared my throat. What did sound good? Hmmmmm. Oh, I wanted pad thai!

"How about a Thai place?" I suggested, and FeeDee nodded.

A few minutes later, she was leading me into a restaurant closer to downtown called Barrel and Squid on Congress Street. It sat next to a tall apartment building and a used bookstore called Blue Hand Bookshop.

The right side of the restaurant was lined with individual tables and a booth that must have been 20 feet long. A wide table and stools sat under the shop's front window for customers to eat and people-watch. In the back of the restaurant, a television playing one of the newer *Star Wars* films hung from the ceiling. And underneath it was a sushi bar.

Our server took us to the furthest table still

attached to the right-side booth, and I sat in a chair on one side while FeeDee rested her back against the wall.

Opposite us hung a massive wooden clock that I kind of wanted to take and hang in my living room.

The smell of sushi and cooking rice filled the restaurant air around us. And it wasn't long before I had a large plate of pad thai in front of me. Steam rose from the rice noodles, peanuts, scrambled eggs, bean sprouts, and the rest of my stir-fried platter, and I inhaled it like a cartoon character lifted into the air by a pie on a windowsill.

Three bites in, I finally clocked back into reality and glanced over at the large platter of orange chicken, steamed carrots, broccoli, and green beans in front of my date.

"Doing better?" I asked after a few more bites of food.

All FeeDee could manage was a few yummy in her tummy noises as her mouth was full and locked behind a big, satisfied smile.

An older couple came in and was seated at a table behind us. They were chatting about their Airbnb, and I saw Frankie roll her eyes.

"Oh, hey, before I forget. I got you a present," the newspaper editor said, pulling her purse closer and handing me a wrapped gift. The paper covering the box was filled with wands and black cats. It was wrapped perfectly, too. No creases or loose edges. On my best day, I could NEVER manage something like this.

"You didn't have to do that," I said, taking the box-shaped gift about the size of my hand.

"Yeah, but I wanted to," she said, shrugging.

Carefully opening the present, I was greeted with a box of tarot cards wrapped in thin plastic. The deck was simply called Newsprint Tarot. And. . . the sight of it stole my breath away. This faithful Catholic had gone out and found a tarot deck to give me for my birthday.

I opened the box and looked through the cards, my eye stopping on the Two of Wands. The wands were rolled up newspapers with rubber bands tying them tight. The rest of the art was full of blacks, grays, and whites. Drawing The Fool, I was greeted with an illustration of a fedora with a press badge stuck in the rim floating in a large puddle.

The next card I drew was Justice, and it featured a front-page news story of some SCOTUS ruling with newsprint artwork of a set of scales and a blindfolded woman holding them high.

"Frankie. . .," I started and ran my fingers over the deck. "This is beautiful."

She smiled and reached her hand across the table to take my free palm.

"I'm glad you like it. I wasn't sure if there were any sacred witch rules about how you had to receive tarot decks."

I snorted.

"I'd be more worried about breaking some Catholic rules by buying one of these," I said, looking down at our hands. Her grip was warm and felt like everything I wanted on a night I expected to be alone.

"Eh, don't worry about it. I'll just slip Father Carlos a $20 on Sunday and buy an indulgence," she said, shrugging her shoulders.

I gave her a blank stare.

"Like — with Pope Leo? Buying forgiveness? The Protestant Reformation? Eh, forget it, bub. It's just some dated Catholic humor for ya."

I shook my head.

"Hard tellin' not knowin', I guess," I laughed.

Frankie Dee lightly tapped my leg with her shoe and rolled her eyes.

Our server came by to refill our drinks, and to my surprise, FeeDee still kept our fingers held loosely together.

Wait. . . if she's holding my hand in front of others. . ., I started to think before we were handed the bill, and Frankie paid it with a translucent credit card.

Finishing my dinner and gently slipping the gift into my purse, I said, "FeeDee. . . the gift is perfect. Thank you."

She winked at me.

"You're welcome, Summers."

She winked at me?! Who was I sitting across the table from right now? Had a monster from a John Carpenter movie taken Frankie's place?

Either way, my heart was playing a game of hopscotch. I pulled the collar on my dress and took a drink of my water.

Frankie just giggled and said, "You ready to go?"

I nodded.

We walked slowly, but Frankie led us down Congress Street until we turned down Exchange and headed into the Old Port.

"What's next on your agenda for my birthday kidnapping?" I asked, and Frankie pointed her chin at a little place called MDIce Cream.

My regular stomach was filled with noodles, but my dessert stomach was still plenty empty. Most scientists will tell you the human body only has one stomach. And they're partially right. Except for being completely wrong. We actually have two separate stomachs, one for meals and one for sweets. That explains how we always have room for dessert after a huge supper. They'd figure it out someday.

While we waited in line, a couple of screaming children ran in circles while their tired and miserable-looking parents ignored them, staring at their phones. I clutched my fists and muttered, *Goddamned crotch goblins.*

We eventually walked out of the ice cream shop. I'd gotten a scoop of rocky road while resisting the urge to give my date shit for only getting plain vanilla. We both licked our waffle cones and walked down Commercial Street, weaving between tourists.

Neither of us said much, just enjoying the evening breeze as we passed pier after pier. Our path led us by the Narrow Gauge Railroad and empty train cars with "No Trespassing" signs on them.

Frankie held her hand out, and I took it as we finished our ice cream and tossed the napkins into a green trash can.

Plenty of folks were out riding bikes or rollerblading down the Eastern Promenade Trail. It wrapped around the peninsula and led to East End Beach.

We walked by stone benches and stared out at the ocean, Fort Gorges looming across the harbor. Our eyes drifted over Bug Light and Peaks Island in the distance. A yellow and white ferry was slowly working its way back toward the harbor.

Without any real planning, we found ourselves sitting on a stone bench above some large rocks. Every few seconds, they were splashed with waves that came in. The sky was painted with hues of pink and soft red.

Seagulls screamed above us, and the sea breeze rattled the trees and bushes that seemed to seclude us from the trail.

We sat there for several minutes, and my head found Frankie's shoulder again. She shivered a little, though I couldn't tell if it was from the wind or my touch.

"FeeDee. . . thank you."

"No problem, bub," she said as we both stared out over the water. And somehow. . . my words weren't enough. It was as though I wasn't expressing the depth of my true love and gratitude for this night.

I lifted my head, and our eyes found each other. Our faces close. . . so fucking close.

"No, Frankie, listen. I was fully prepared to spend tonight alone with a bottle of wine and *Godzilla vs. Gigan*. But you heard I had no birthday plans, scrapped your work schedule, and rode to my rescue. You took me dancing, you bought me dinner, you gave me the most magical gift, and then you just let me meander with ice cream."

Frankie Dee giggled.

"You do love to meander," she said.

I grabbed her chin.

"No! Listen to me. Stop trying to joke these feelings away. This isn't Canaan House, and you're not wearing Aviators."

She froze. I'm pretty sure I could see her heart rattling behind those wide dinner-plate eyes, even if FeeDee had no clue what I was talking about. I could estimate her heart rate because mine was probably close to doubling it. Still, I took a deep breath and moved my face closer.

"This has been the greatest birthday I've ever had, and it's all thanks to you. So please don't misunderstand. I am not merely thankful, Frankie, as if you'd fixed my flat tire or loaned me a book.

I'm moved nearly beyond words. I'm happier in this moment than I can remember being in a long time, and you did that. So acknowledge my fucking raw feelings, or I'll push you into the tide."

Before I could say another word, Frankie ran her fingers across my cheek, and I swear I could see her eyes quivering. Those walnut-colored eyes quaked as we both stood at the ever-fraying line between us. Promises. Questions. Desires. They all hung suspended in the air around us, ready to fly high or come crashing down upon two girls who were so deep in their feelings that drowning was no longer optional, or even unwanted.

With her warm breath mere inches from my lips, Frankie asked, "Summers. . . what are we?"

And I sensed that here and now, I had a chance to cut through this boundary once and for all. This was a moment where I'd been given a chisel, separated from my greatest wants and needs by a mere thin wall of stone. One swing would bring it all down.

Perhaps what was most terrifying about the feelings racing through my chest was that they were all overshadowed by a sudden, growing realization in my mind. I had no clue what lay on the other side of that boundary.

I might get everything I've ever wanted. Or I might scare the girl of my dreams and leave our relationship a broken mess. She liked me, right?

This wasn't the kind of shit you did for a friend, even a bestie.

This was, "my heart would travel through 5,000 suns just to be near you" kind of love. . . right? But what if it only led to regret for this woman I'd only known for a couple of months? What was better, to stay here in this warm and undefined space where we could continue with vague happiness or to take the risk of pushing for more, knowing it could break the space I've come to crave?

Fuck, I thought, freezing.

And I found myself thinking back to Emma's email of all things, her question that I didn't want to answer. My brain chose a path before I even realized what I was saying.

"Intertwined souls," I whispered. "We're a couple of intertwined souls."

Then I laid my head upon her shoulder again, providing a vague witchy answer and feeling like nothing short of a coward. But gods be damned. I just couldn't risk giving up what we had. Somehow, in our time together, it'd come to mean everything to me. I didn't want that space to fade away like so many other things I'd lost in my life.

15

(Frankie)

I'd just finished salting the rims of my wide blue glasses when a knock sounded on the front door. Walking out of my kitchenette, I strode across the soft white carpeted floor to greet my guest.

Stretching my shoulders and back like a cat against the doorframe before opening it, I sighed quietly.

You vacuumed, dusted, and washed the dishes, I thought. *You're fine. Stop panicking.*

While my brain tried to stage a coup over the fact that I ran out of time to mop the kitchen floor, I pushed that aside and opened the front door to find Dawn standing on my front porch with a plastic shopping bag.

"My, my, Summers. What did you bring me?" I asked.

"Chips and salsa. And maybe if your margaritas

are as strong as you say they are, we can have dessert too."

I crossed my arms.

"You got something in the bag for that as well?"

Locking eyes with me, the witch confidently and quietly said, "no," before walking past me inside my little guest house.

I shivered as Dawn's fingers lightly brushed my bare arm.

My eyes traced across the yard to the main house where my parents stayed. Through the back patio window, I spotted Mom and Dad putting a puzzle together on the dinner table. If they saw Dawn come over, they didn't make any move to reveal that.

They're good actors, I thought, rolling my eyes before closing the front door.

My living room was the biggest part of the guest house I called home, filled with a black leather couch and a navy recliner I salvaged from a nearby thrift shop called Little Specter.

Gray curtains covered all my windows, and I closed them, clicking on my floor lamp and adding more light to the living room.

"Cute little place you've got here," Dawn said, looking at some framed article clippings I had on the wall from our paper. Only one was written by me. Franky Jr. and my grandfather, Franky Sr., had penned the others. They'd picked up their share of regional journalism awards for covering things like school budget fraud and a cargo ship crash in the Portland Harbor back in '72.

I went to the kitchen and brought over our margaritas.

"Thank you," I said, setting them on a long table in front of the sofa.

"I especially like the Amtrak clock you've got hanging on the wall. That looks vintage," she said.

And where I expected her to poke fun at my decor, I was stunned to see genuine interest from the witch.

"Th—thanks," I stammered, caught off guard. "That's actually the logo introduced in 1971. They ran it until the late '90s. So many of the trains and coaches were painted with red and blue stripes, accompanied by a narrow white line in the center."

Dawn took a sip of the margarita I'd mixed, and she nodded, licking some of the extra salt that traced her lips. God, what I'd give for her to be licking me like a margarita glass. Shit had gotten so mixed up these last few weeks, ever since Boston. My thoughts were increasingly out of control.

And the witch was pushing past the boundaries I established on Mackworth Island. She'd stop in an instant if I said something, but I never managed to muster the energy to speak up. Did I want her to quit?

A journalist's job is to report the facts. I huffed. The facts, as I knew them, were that I was desperate for her to keep pushing past the line I'd drawn in the sand. There was nothing more I craved than for Dawn to scatter that line as she ravished me with every ounce of magic she could muster.

Fuck, I'm down bad, I thought.

What was stopping me from telling her this? I was 99 percent sure she'd jump my bones here and now if I told her that's what I wanted. I'd unexpectedly given her the space to do just that on her birthday.

Last week, with everything in my chest quivering, I'd asked her what we were. And she chose not to dash over the line I'd drawn and bring her lips to mine like I was so desperately craving. Did she not pick up on that? Goddammit. How deeply did I have to look into her eyes for her to see my longing? Truly, I thought, nothing was more obvious than what I wanted from her.

If my life was a romance novel, I'd accuse the author of having no legitimate reason to keep us apart other than to draw up the fucking tension. But she'd have to be a real bitch to do such an awful thing.

"I never knew you were such a train enthusiast," Dawn said, glancing at the clock again.

Pulled out of my thoughts, I cleared my throat.

"Oh, yeah. Well, it's not all trains. Just passenger rail."

"Yeah?"

"Mmmmhhmmmm," I nodded. "You see, the Downeaster we rode isn't even a quarter of a century old yet. From 1965 to 2001, there was no passenger rail between Portland and Boston. But rumblings to resurrect it started in the '90s courtesy of a series of editorials my father penned. After a few years, voters urged the Legislature to act, approving funding, and creating a railroad authority for the state. Dad has pictures of state senators reading his editorials in Augusta before each vote. Anyway, when the Downeaster made its inaugural run, he was on that train. And Mom bought him that clock to celebrate."

Dawn whistled.

"Damn, girl. You have any idea how cute it is for you to infodump?"

I rolled my eyes for the second time in 10 minutes.

"Shut up and put the DVD in the player while I get a bowl for the tortilla chips."

The witch walked over toward the TV.

"Can't we just eat out of the bag?"

"No, because we aren't savages," I called from the kitchen, pulling a Xena: Warrior Princess popcorn bowl from a cabinet above the fridge.

Dawn was reading the back of the DVD case when I came back into the living room.

"*The Paper*? Is this part of my journalism lesson for tonight?" she asked, raising an eyebrow. "How old is this movie?"

I giggled.

"Older than either of us. From a magical year

called 1994. And, yes, it's part of tonight's lesson. So you can spot the difference between Hollywood journalism and what actually happens at the newspaper."

She crossed her arms.

"You stole my lesson! Cheater," Dawn huffed.

"As if I'd ever cheat on you," I scoffed before my brain could stop to realize what I'd just said.

For a moment, I thought I'd lucked out and maybe the witch didn't hear me. She put the DVD into the player and stood up while the TV changed from a blue screen to one of those stupid FBI anti-piracy warnings everyone ignored.

But then she swung those deep emerald eyes around my way, I felt my world go sideways. All I could do was stare, helpless in her gaze.

"I know you wouldn't, dear. The last girl who cheated on me regretted it immediately. I hexed her to have two periods every month. The spell was so powerful, I'm fairly certain she has to take iron supplements now."

I shuddered at the threat, unsure of whether Dawn was joking or even truly capable of such a thing. A journalist's job is to find the facts. And the facts were. . . I still didn't know jack shit about witchcraft, and I was scared to learn anymore.

"So. . . what is *The Paper* about?"

"Batman runs a newspaper," I said, sitting down on the couch and taking a drink of my margarita.

Dawn looked at the cover again.

"Robert Pattinson was a child in 1994," she said, frowning and flipping it over to stare at the names on the back.

I groaned.

"The old Batman."

"Oh shit. Is Ben Affleck in this movie?"

"No, the one before him."

"No way. That dude on the cover is too old to be Christian Bale," Dawn said, tossing it on the table and pouring her chips into my bowl.

Taking another drink, I nearly choked.

When I could breathe clearly, I said, "Not those Batmen. Michael Keaton."

"Who?" she asked and I shook my head, starting the movie.

Dawn plopped herself down next to me, our hips touching, and she placed her feet on the table.

"You care?" she asked, looking at me.

I shook my head.

"Mi casa su casa," I said, dipping a chip in some salsa.

Dawn giggled and muttered, "Eh, give it another week or two."

We watched Keaton shine on the camera with a powerful cast behind him, teaching the audience about the value of a newspaper and how journalism serves its readers.

By the time the credits rolled, Dawn had her head on my shoulders again, and we'd finished half the pitcher of margaritas.

"What's next?" the witch asked, rousing herself from the lull of watching our movie together.

"I got *The Post*," I said, standing up too quickly and feeling an uncomfortably familiar twinge in my chest.

What is it going to take for you to fucking stop that? I thought, scowling.

While Dawn poured the last of the chips into the bowl, she asked, "What's this one about?"

"Ummmm. Tom Hanks and Meryl Streep run *The Washington Post*. It's a little grandiose, but some of their scenes together are just too good to hate. Some folks called it Oscar bait, but I enjoyed it. It's no *Spotlight*, but it's still pretty good."

We started the film, and my eyes were getting so damn heavy. It was only 9:30 p.m., but I'd been on my feet for most of the day touring new paper mill upgrades for a business story out of Rumford. The CEO had actually flown into Bangor from Hong Kong, and I snagged an interview this afternoon.

I accidentally brushed my foot against the leg of my table and grimaced, worn nerves firing off up and down my foot.

"Goddammit," I mumbled.

"You good, FeeDee?"

"Fine," I said, shifting my hips a little.

The witch looked down at my feet and then back at my squinting eyes.

"Feet sore from the mill tour? You were gone all day, weren't you?" Dawn asked.

How the fuck did she know that? I thought. *Is she able to read my mind? Can witches do that?*

Cutting right through my panic, Dawn shifted down to the far end of the sofa away from me. Then she did the unexpected and pulled my feet into her lap.

"What are you doing?!" I hissed.

"Quit fussing. Teach me something about journalism. What's happening right now?" she asked.

I was torn between scolding her and talking at length about the Pentagon Papers when Dawn's fingers gripped the back of my foot, and her thumbs found my tightened tendons, applying a bit of pressure.

"Oh. . . my god," I hissed, letting out a stream of air and leaning back onto the arm of my sofa. "Summers, you need to —"

She interrupted me.

"Keep going? I agree. Your feet are pulled tighter than guitar strings. Get some insoles, girl."

The witch ran her thumbs from the arch of my foot to an inch short of my toes, and I let out a soft moan as endorphins flooded my brain, washing away any remaining protest I had. And, let's be honest, I didn't have any real protest of substance. It was all bluster.

Why do you do that? I asked myself, failing to come up with an answer.

My nervous system was lit with the simultaneous shivers and fireworks of Dawn's fingerwork, and I collapsed backward, unable to muster any real comment or further protest on my two hours of sleep.

"Okay. . . you win. Please keep going," I mumbled.

"As you wish," the witch said in her best Cary Elwes impression.

When the movie was half over, and I was half asleep, I suddenly spoke up.

"You know, Dad had the chance to work for the *Washington Post*, not long after Franky Sr. died, and Dad inherited the *Lighthouse-Journal*."

Dawn was working on my other foot now, and my leg and toes were twitching in joy as I still occasionally caught myself making involuntary noises of pleasure. Maybe even an expletive or two.

"Goddammit, you're good with those hands, Summers."

Without missing a beat, she said, "Imagine what I could do with them elsewhere, not just on FeeDee's feeties."

I grimaced.

"Never say those words together again, please."

"As you wish," she said, again, winking. "Did Franky Jr. move to Washington?"

Slowly, I shook my head.

"He didn't take the job?"

"Dad didn't even interview for it. He politely declined the plane ticket to fly down there to even meet with the editors."

"Isn't the *Post* — like — one of the most prestigious papers in the country?"

Shrugging, I turned my eyes away from the television and down to the witch who was being sweet enough to stick in a pie.

Hanks and Streep were in her office discussing the ramifications of publishing classified material, and I just kept picturing my dad on the phone, with a soft but firm "No thank you," for the newspaper editors in our capital.

"He uh. . . never really wanted to leave. When I was 16 and covering my first city council meetings, I asked him why. I was sure I would have taken that job if it were offered to me. It sounded crazy to turn down such an opportunity."

Dawn didn't interrupt me. She just waited for the rest of the story.

"And God bless him, my dad just looked me straight in the eye and said, 'These are our readers, FeeDee. And it's my job to inform them of all the important news happening in their community.'

"He didn't care that his writing would reach millions of eyeballs if it was published in the Sunday edition of the *Post*. What mattered more to him was telling his barber, his school teachers, his lobstermen, and every other subscriber about road closures, millage votes, utility rate increases, and more. The awards and prestige never meant a damn to my old man. He just didn't want any

Mainers to be left with questions they needed answered."

Dawn smiled at me and said, "Now those are your readers. And you're the one who would turn down the Washington job if it was offered to you."

My eyes drooped low.

"I've turned down editor jobs in Boston and New York. This is my home, bub. This is my paper. I sweat and bleed ink every day to keep our readers informed. They gotta know, Summers. They always have the right to know," I said, my voice trailing off.

"And you'll tell them," she said, softly, pulling a fuzzy blanket from the back of the couch and tucking us in, burying her face in my chest as my mind finally surrendered to the endorphin-fueled darkness that held me.

That night, I dreamed of Michael Keaton sitting me down in his office and asking why a flirty headline about a certain witch had made it to print. And I wasn't even the least bit ashamed.

"Thirty thousand readers saw this on their front page this morning!" he snapped.

"And I wanted them all to know," I said, shortly before being fired.

I awoke to my television's blue screen and the DVD tray ejected from its player. Sunlight was mostly hidden behind the gray curtains on my living room windows.

Dawn was already awake and turned her eyes

up to me. Though I suspect, she hadn't been up for long.

"How the fuck does this keep happening?" I asked.

She shrugged.

"Do you want me to go?" she asked.

"I want . . .," I mumbled, stretching backward.

"Yeah?" she prodded.

My vision cleared, and her soft green eyes were looking up at mine as if waiting for the most important answer in the world. And damn me if all I could tell her was, "I want to start a pot of coffee."

16

(Frankie)

All around me, men and women in tuxedos and fancy dresses filled the convention center turned banquet hall. Streamers and decorations hung from the ceiling lit by three large chandeliers. Polished tile floor waited for dancers as the Greater Portland Symphony kept the wealthy guests company, along with bottomless flutes of champagne and wine.

I was hiding out by the kitchen staff entrance near an abandoned coat rack and waiting for my chest to stop feeling like a balloon about to pop. The pressure that'd built up was sending twinges of pain through my arms, and I wanted nothing more than to go home and sleep for five years, maybe 10.

Of course, sleep would have to wait. Right now, I was supervising Craig and introducing him to some important people to build his networking and sources for future stories. Plenty of important people had shown up for the gala that served as a fundraiser for Southern Maine Children's Hospital.

I'd already taken Craig over to the president of the Portland Chamber of Commerce, the vice president of the Maine Realtors Association, the Cumberland County Fishermens Union press secretary, and three other names that'd slipped my mind when the room started to spin.

My phone chimed, and a text from Dawn immediately brought a smile to my face.

"Where are you?" she'd asked.

I smirked.

"Helping Craig cover the hospital gala," I responded.

The little dancing bubbles popped up at the bottom of our text message as she typed something back.

"I'm pretty sure you skipped lunch again. Wanna grab dinner after the rich people finish earning their tax write-offs for the year?" she texted.

I snickered and told her yes. This was the third night this week we'd eaten dinner together. Before I could ask myself an obvious question about how much time we were spending together,

another arc of pain seized my chest, and threatened to split it like an almond in a nutcracker. I took three narrow breaths, all I could manage at the moment, and attempted to will the pain away.

Grit and spite had kept me going through my

most exhausted moments, and I didn't expect them to fail me now.

"C'mon. Pipe down. I've got work to do," I growled.

A few men in black tuxedos exited the kitchen carrying silver trays with little sandwiches on them. Then, a woman wearing the same staff outfit walked past with a tray of shrimp cocktails. She paused to look at me.

"Are you okay, ma'am?" she asked with a surprisingly thick southern drawl.

Where are you from? I thought before offering a hand in the air to gesture that I was fine.

"Just taking a breather," I said with a smile.

The staff member was about to say something else when one of her coworkers called her name. Then, she sped off to find the others who had been carrying food.

Just before I grew desperate enough to throw up my white flag of surrender and finally tell someone about my chest pain, it crept away, back into the recesses of wherever it hid in between my pitiful sleep schedule and abysmal diet.

"Okay," I breathed, feeling the room slowly stop spinning. "We can do this. Just make sure Craig meets a few more people, takes a few more photos, and then we can go back to the newsroom so he can write his story about the gala."

I wasn't sure who I was talking to. Maybe I just needed to reassure myself of the night to come.

Replaying my schedule before my eyes told me there were still items on today's checklist to take care of before I could crash and sleep like my body so desperately wanted.

When a staff member came by, I pulled him over and said, "Can you please grab me a hot coffee?"

He nodded and returned with exactly that.

I poured the liquid caffeine down my throat and into the stomach which hadn't seen food since this afternoon's bag of BBQ chips.

"Okay, let's do this," I said, stepping away from my hiding spot and nearly colliding with an older man wearing a gray designer suit that probably cost more than my parents' house. His grayish-blue eyes scanned me, and I suddenly felt like a gazelle being eyed by a hungry lion.

"Yes, let's do this," he said, extending a hand. "I'm—"

I interrupted him.

"I know who you are, Mr. Cutlow."

Rage filled my chest, and I struggled to breathe again, though this time because I was worried about exhaling a stream of pure fire on the man whose calls I'd been ignoring for the past few days.

"Can't blame me for being a little paranoid you'd forgotten me. You haven't taken any more of my calls, Ms. Ricci," he said, taking his hand back when it was clear I wasn't going to shake it.

Fuck, I hated the way he said my last name.

"When I decline your offers and calls, it's because I've decided we have nothing to chat about."

"And when I continue to press forward with my hunt, it's because I've decided we do have something to chat about, namely, your failing newspaper that will soon become my successful, efficient, and profitable publication."

I crossed my arms and scowled.

"Did you think I'd have a harder time refusing your offer in person?" I asked, grinding the front of my black heels into the tile and wishing the friction would start a fire to separate us.

Mr. Cutlow stood five inches taller than me and with the poise of a man who wasn't told no often. And if he was, it wasn't a "no" for very long.

His mustache was trimmed, his nails well manicured, and the Rolex watch on his wrist nice and tight. The man's jacket was buttoned up and drowning in cologne.

From a distance, Mr. Cutlow might be mistaken for William Hurt, and I'm sure he loved it when that happened.

"I thought perhaps you'd come to see reason if we shared drinks, danced a couple of times, and talked numbers."

Fuck me, I need more time, I thought. It'd be at least another few weeks before I had the newest quarter's subscriber numbers in my hands and could prove my plan to bring Dawn's audience over to our newspaper was successful.

But lions don't work on your schedule. They work on their tummy's timetable and hunt when they're hungry. And Mr. Cutlow looked positively ravenous for my family's newspaper.

"You really drove the five hours from Manhatten just to sweet-talk me into giving you the Lighthouse-Journal?" I asked.

"Don't flatter yourself, Ms. Ricci. My yacht has been docked in the harbor for three days now. I've been visiting some friends on Peaks Island and looking at Portland's real estate market. Imagine my surprise when those same friends told me about a gala tonight, and I saw your name on the guest list."

I scoffed.

"Great, so it's not just my newspaper you're after but probably the family home of some poor blue-collar workers that are being priced out of Portland by assholes like you, buying up all the affordable housing and raising rents to obscene levels."

And where I expected Mr. Cutlow to sigh or roll his eyes, he didn't. The man just took in a sharp breath and reached out to grab another glass of champagne from a nearby tray.

The dance floor in the next room had its first visitors as an older couple slowly swayed left and right. I think one of them was the county accessor.

Mr. Cutlow lowered his voice.

"You know, Ms. Ricci, I actually admire how hard you've fought for your publication. You've got all the makings of a scrappy underdog fighting off the evil corporate giant coming to claim something your family spent years building."

"Thanks, bub. That's quite a compliment," I said, arms still crossed.

The investor scratched his neck.

"You and I are just two people chasing after our wants. We see the same things from different perspectives. You look at your newspaper and see a valuable community resource that keeps this little city up to date on everything from local elections to whoever wins teacher of the year. I look at your newspaper and see a tool that can be trimmed, tailored, and tossed into a money basket with the rest of Aidan Global Capital's 27 publications."

My blood pressure kept finding new ceilings to shatter as I pictured 27 family newspapers that'd been ripped from their communities and stripped for parts, left hollow and bereft of good stories and photographs.

"If I sold you my newspaper, you'd lay off half the staff, slash insurance benefits, and reduce coverage this community desperately needs."

The man in front of me didn't scowl or laugh. He just kept staring, waiting patiently for me to finish speaking.

With another sharp breath, Mr. Cutlow said, "Without a doubt, Ms. Ricci. While you fight hard to protect your family's legacy, I watch the market every second of every day, looking for food my company can gobble up. I like my yacht, Ms. Ricci. I like my jet. I like my three vacation homes. I like my private box for New York Nyx games. And I like making my shareholders happy."

Out of the corner of my eye, I spotted Craig raising a camera to his eyes to photograph some of the dancers. Then, I turned my attention back to Mr. Cutlow.

"Shouldn't you be telling me some bullshit story about wanting to keep journalism alive and rescuing struggling newspapers in a dying industry?"

The investor standing before me took a long drink of his champagne and shook his head.

"What's the point of lying to you, Ms. Ricci? You're intelligent. Your writing is sharp. And your news instincts render any story I could throw your way absolutely worthless. Hell, you're probably smarter than I am. But you're missing one important thing."

I raised an eyebrow.

"What am I missing?"

"Money. You could be the smartest person in the room, but if I hire five PhDs, you're outmatched. You could be the strongest person in the room, but if I pay 20 bodybuilders, you're outgunned. And you can fight all day long to keep your newspaper out of Aidan Global Capital's hands. But eventually, you'll run out of resources, and it'll wind up in our portfolio regardless."

In truth, I found his lack of threats and bullshit disturbing. Mr. Cutlow spoke about inevitabilities and had the hard data to back up his claims.

He wasn't some Saturday morning cartoon villain coming to give his monologue and lose in the final five minutes of the episode.

While my brain told me to hold fast and keep the line steady, I instead found my resolve crumbling. My knees wanted to buckle and find a chair to sit in. And perhaps I'd damned myself with only getting two hours of sleep last night. But Mr. Cutlow was a vicious opponent no matter how well-rested I was.

And let's say I got everything I wanted. He left tonight. My subscription numbers showed a sharp increase thanks to Dawn's efforts. And I got a little breathing room for my newspaper and myself. What happened next? How long could I breathe before the next inevitable challenge came down the pike? Even if my newspaper overperformed for a quarter or two, the industry as a whole wasn't going to change anytime soon.

Press parts were becoming more difficult to find. Newsprint and ink were only getting more expensive. And every year, our insurance company wanted to charge more and cover less. Fuck, I was tired.

Was there some tiny shred of my mind that

wanted to take a large check from Mr. Cutlow and sleep for the next five years? Or had exhaustion simply robbed me of reason this fine and expensive night? Maybe I was just tired of carrying all these burdens alone. Where was my Magic 8 Ball?

With every bit of stubborn resolve I could muster, I paused and looked the investor square in the eyes before saying, "My newspaper is not for sale, Mr. Cutlow. In six hours, our printing press will start firing up. And we'll have a front-page story about our school's superintendent being fired over financial misconduct allegations. The masthead at the top of the paper will list Frankie Dee Ricci as managing editor and Ricci Press Inc. as the owners, not Aidan Global Capital. I don't expect the masthead to change anytime soon. God willing, my future daughter's name will replace mine someday. But your company's name will never have a space in my publication, not while I'm still breathing."

Mr. Cutlow rubbed his chin and finished his champagne, putting the empty glass on a nearby table decorated with napkins folded like swans.

"Like I said, Ms. Ricci. I admire how hard you're fighting for the Lighthouse-Journal. I'll leave you be for the night. But I do have one final warning before I go."

My chest tightened.

"A warning?"

He stepped back, putting space between us.

"Not about your paper. My younger brother,

you see, loves to golf. And he loves his beer, ribs, and brisket. Not a big fan of greens or water. Well, greens outside of the course, I mean."

At this, Mr. Cutlow chuckled and shook his head.

I was left standing in a puddle of confusion.

"Sorry — my point being, my younger brother isn't the healthiest man. He's survived two heart attacks, though. See? Money helps a lot of things. Doctors. Surgeries. Prescriptions. You can live dumb and make poor choices when you have it. But in the weeks before he collapsed, both times in the fairway hunting for his ball, and was rushed to the emergency room, he clutched his chest like you were doing a few minutes ago."

A shiver raced down my spine. The sounds of my father being loaded into a stretcher and an ambulance racing down Congress Street echoed in the back of my ears. I struggled to remember to breathe as it felt like every time I inhaled, most of the air snagged somewhere in my throat, not quite reaching my lungs.

"You're half his age, Ms. Ricci. But you're working twice as hard as my little brother. My guess? This newspaper you're fighting so hard to cling to is slowly killing you. I'd never presume to tell you how to live your life. But if I were in your shoes, I'd be asking if my family's business was worth dying for. Enjoy the party, Ms. Ricci. You've got my number if you change your mind."

With that final warning, Mr. Cutlow left and went to speak with the owner of three different restaurants here in Portland, none of which I could afford to eat at.

My hands were shaking as I retreated back to the coat rack. I took shallow breaths and tried to will away, not pain this time, but fear. I didn't want to imagine there was anything wrong with me. Because if I gave into that fear, something might actually BE wrong with me. It'd be like manifesting my worst nightmare.

No — the rules for my health were simple. If I didn't look directly at my problems, they couldn't bother me. They were like apparitions trapped behind glass. As long as they weren't acknowledged, they were ultimately powerless.

Armed with this newfound, albeit shaky reassurance, I wandered back into the main hall. The dance floor was absolutely packed down.

Two older men who I recognized as the COO and CFO of the children's hospital posed in front of an ice sculpture, shaking hands and looking at Craig's camera with drunken grins plastered on their faces.

The young reporter eventually found me.

"Hey, Boss."

"Don't call me that," I groaned.

"Sorry, Boss. I got the quotes I needed. Are we thinking the story should be about 30 inches?"

I shook my head.

"Twenty inches will be plenty. Are you ready to head back to the newsroom?"

He nodded.

"Let's go, then."

A woman's voice spoke up behind me as someone grabbed my arm and slowly spun me around.

"Hold on, there. You can't leave yet. The gala is just getting started, and we have so much catching up to do."

As a gorgeous woman with long shiny black hair came into view, I couldn't help but eye the lime halter mini dress clinging to her body, her legs (for days), her matching flats, and her million-dollar smile. A face I used to kiss and make giggle stood just inches from mine. Wide brown eyes searched my own and drank every bit of the surprise she found in my gaze.

For the third time tonight, my heart seized, and once again for a different reason.

Margaret. . . fuck, I thought, trying not to show her the dread that was spreading through my stomach like tree roots under a forest.

"Hello, FeeDee. Long time, no see," my ex-girlfriend said. I noticed her hand was still touching my elbow.

I was struggling for a greeting. What did you say to a woman who broke your heart and left you pouring all your remaining love and passion into work so you didn't have to think about the pain she left you with? Maybe there wasn't a simple word to describe that. It was a pretty specific situation I'd been left in.

"FeeDee?" Craig asked behind me.

"Don't call me that," I said without looking at the young pup of a reporter. "Go back to calling me 'Boss.'"

"Yes, Boss," he said and immediately made himself scarce.

I tried to summon a frown for the woman who'd left me without warning, but a low-pressure system had settled over my brain, bringing flooding and painful memories with it.

"And you don't call me that either," I said.

Margaret watched as I took a step away from her, pulling out of her grasp.

"I'm glad you came," she said. And I noticed her nails were painted the same color as her dress. The hospital marketing executive always loved her salons.

But when you're in the job of communicating for a nonprofit that rakes in millions of dollars each year, it helps to look pretty, she'd told me two or three times.

It wasn't that Margaret was unintelligent. On the contrary, she was smart enough to know older rich men are more likely to buy gala tickets and make hospital donations when asked by a young lady with a pretty face and killer tits. She was also smart enough to know that being a television reporter (or an MMJ as it was called in the industry) came with shit hours and even shittier pay. So, she found a better use for her degree in communications and was much happier for it.

"I'm here because of work," I said, managing to chill my voice just a hair.

She shrugged, ignoring my displeasure.

"Regardless, you're here, and I'm happy to see you."

"I wish I could say the same," I said. "Now, if you'll excuse me, I've got to get back to the newsroom. Good luck with the auction later tonight."

Margaret's long nails lightly grabbed my elbow again.

"Hey now. We haven't spoken in months. Don't you wanna tell me what you've been up to?"

Working myself toward a heart attack, apparently, I thought, glumly, thinking back to Mr. Cutlow's words. Fucking hell, I couldn't catch a break tonight.

"Working, working, and more working. Not much to tell," I said, my thoughts suddenly flying to a certain witch who'd been spending an inordinate amount of time with me over the last month.

Margaret tucked a strand of my blonde hair behind my ear, and I flinched. She'd made a habit of doing that when we were together.

"So, I can see your pretty walnut eyes when you tell me about your latest article," she'd always say.

Her eyes looked me up and down.

"That's a cute shirt and trousers," she said.

I shook my head.

"What are you doing, Margaret?" I asked.

She cocked her head to the side a little before answering. It sent part of her hair cascading over a bare shoulder. A shoulder I used to caress in her condo after two or three glasses of wine and a stressful deadline at work.

I closed my eyes and tried to shove those thoughts to the side.

"I'm talking to someone I haven't seen in a while. And you're acting like I'm carrying a dagger behind my back."

She showed me both hands.

"See? No blade. Just an old friend who. . . fucked up and hurt someone dear to her."

Margaret's eyes were looking at the floor when she started that sentence, and they slowly lifted to my gaze by the end of her words. My mind fluttered, and I reached around for something sturdy to grab. In a panic, I found nothing, and Margaret rushed forward to steady me.

Being in her arms again, smelling my ex's chocolate pistachio body lotion left me wanting to cry, to run in the opposite direction, and to somehow apologize for scaring her off, even though that was total bullshit.

Was I starving and exhausted, or did I actually miss Margaret? The way she used to bake little chocolate chip cookies and bring them to my office, the Mariah Carey songs she'd hum in the shower, and the awful Hallmark movies we had to watch during each holiday. All of it came rushing back.

And just before I lowered my head onto her shoulder and sank further into Margaret's embrace, her words came back to me, screeching in my mind.

"I'm sorry, Frankie. That's just not what I want for us," she'd said.

Images flashed through my brain like lightning, the ring I'd bought to propose, the reservation for our celebration dinner after she (would've) said yes, and the wedding venues my mother would want to book. Except it all shattered like a hammer striking a lightbulb.

"N — no," I uttered, weakly, stepping away from Margaret. "You said no."

To her credit, the marketing executive wore a pained expression. Her face showed nothing but regret.

"FeeDee, listen. I fucked up. I saw the ring receipt on the dresser, and I got scared. I didn't think I was ready to get married. And in the storm of my emotions, I hurt you. I'm sorry."

Was I crying? Goddamit. This wasn't what I imagined for tonight. Just 20 minutes ago, I was thinking about where Dawn would want to have dinner. But why shouldn't I have expected the marketing executive for the children's hospital to attend her own company's gala?

Margaret reached into her purse and grabbed

an honest-to-god handkerchief. It was white and embroidered with her family's name "Hutchinson."

Seeing the name brought back memories of the holidays we'd spend at her family's ranch in Wyoming. God, I missed that place. Was I scared of the horses? Sure. But I did love watching Margaret ride. . . from a distance. And her parents were so kind and supportive. I'd been planning on making them my in-laws before everything went all stove up to hell.

I took the handkerchief and wiped the corner of my eyes.

"Okay, fine. You've apologized. I accept your apology," I said. "Really. We're good."

Did I appreciate Marget's words? Yes. Did I think she was being genuine? Also yes. So why couldn't I wait to get away from her? Perhaps there was just still too much pain left over from our breakup for me to want to be in an active conversation with her. And, really, what role did my former partner have in my future? I know the lesbian stereotype is every ex-girlfriend becomes a lifelong buddy relied on for random hookups and future dating advice. But I wasn't sure I could manage that with Marget. Not when I was all-in on our future, and she decided to bail.

My heart throbbed. My throat swelled. And my tears doubled. In hindsight, maybe burying all these feelings and diving headfirst into work wasn't the smartest psychological decision I'd ever made. But hey, therapy is expensive and rarely covered by insurance. Certainly not our insurance.

But I was 100% sure in our relationship. It was a foundation, on which, I intended to build the rest of our lives. And when it crumbled, I ran for the next bedrock I could find, the Lighthouse-Journal. Now, I was in danger of losing that as well.

The men who were photographed earlier were now laughing boisterously at some joke one of the property-management CEOs had told. I closed my eyes again and placed the back of my hand against my forehead.

"I don't just want us to be 'good,' Frankie."

"What do you want?" I asked, with perhaps a little more bite than I intended.

Margaret took a deep breath and pulled me a little closer. I wasn't sure what was happening, but I also didn't have the energy for any more sweeping gestures. I just wanted to be far away from here. Far away from my emotional torment. Or maybe I wanted to be someone's wife, who came home every night to a woman she loved and discussed the day's events with. Perhaps I was tired of overworking myself and arriving home to an empty bed and nobody to cuddle up next to.

I would have had all those things by now if Margaret had been the one for me. But she wasn't. My then-partner had chosen differently. . . hadn't she? What did she say? She got scared?

My life would be wildly different right now if

she hadn't gotten scared. What if I'd waited another six months to propose? We'd talked about getting married, and Margaret made it sound like something she wanted someday. So. . . did I just pick the wrong day?

Her words brought my attention back to the gala.

"I want another chance," she said. And my eyes shot open as far as they would go. "I want what you were planning before I ran like a coward. I want a future with you. Spending holidays at the ranch again. Adopting a daughter together. Growing old in a seaside home that'll probably be washed away a few decades after we kick the bucket courtesy of climate change."

The laugh that snaked its way out of my throat betrayed me. But it was immediately followed by a small sob.

For the first several months after she dumped me, I would have given anything for Margaret Hutchinson to say those words. How many nights did I dream of us sitting next to the fire pit behind the barn on her family's farm in Cody? Mountains dotted with snow under the full moon sky.

At one point, I was even ready to leave Portland and move there to be closer to her family. That's how over the moon I was for this girl. But she was the one who got scared. Not me. She got scared. I got hurt.

"No," I sobbed.

"What?" she asked, genuine hurt flashing on her face. Margaret apparently expected me to just welcome her back if she spilled her guts, and I wasn't having it.

"I would have given you anything you asked for, Maggie. Quit my job. Move across the country. Help take care of your parents in their old age. You were my world. But when I took a step toward our future, a future we both said we wanted, you bolted."

She pulled me over to a side room away from the dancing couples and food tables, not far from the bathrooms. I went with her because, again, I was bushed, physically and now emotionally.

"I know what I said hurt you," she said, placing a hand on my cheek. "But I've changed. I'm not the same person who left you that day in Westbrook."

My bottom lip wobbled, and I shook my head.

"You can't ask me to trust you again, Maggie. You can't. My heart is apparently broken in more ways than one, and I didn't come here tonight expecting to be ambushed like this," I said, trying and failing to stifle my sobs. "Every day, you were my sun that rose high in the sky and promised me everything would be okay. I reveled in your warmth, your radiance, and your life. Even when the clouds came and hid you, I still knew you were there. So imagine my utter heartbreak when I woke up one morning and looked up in the sky to find you'd fled from me."

Now Margaret was tearing up.

"I told you I'm sorry," she said.

"And I forgive you, truly. But I can't trust you not to hurt me again. Not like that. Friends someday? Maybe I can see that. But I will never share a life with you again. Because I just don't think I can survive another heartbreak like the one you left me with."

I couldn't see clearly because of the tears now. And Margaret's handkerchief was soaked.

She ran a couple of fingers through my hair.

"Say I'm not too late. Tell me there's not someone else," she whimpered.

"There's someone else, Maggie. I have a. . . a. . .," my voice trailed off.

"You have a what?" she asked softly.

What did I have? A coworker? A pal? A bestie? In truth, I didn't know what I had. But thinking about Dawn became a balm for my aching heart. I pictured us falling asleep together watching movies, laughing at jokes she made during book club, and walking along the beach together. I didn't know what we had. But I knew I wouldn't trade it to get back together with Margaret, even if she never hurt me again.

A man walked out of the restroom and eyed us before going back into the main room shouting, "Heeeeyyyyyyy! You made it!"

My ex-girlfriend looked at the ground as I heard boots clicking on the floor behind me.

Margaret found her words and said, "Please. . . just—"

She was cut off by a familiar voice taking my elbow and lightly pulling me away from the marketing executive. I sure was spending a lot of tonight literally being pulled in various directions. The woman who now held me cut Margaret off.

"You had your chance. She's with me now."

Turning, I came face-to-face with Dawn. Where had she come from?! I'd told her where I was, but I didn't in a million years expect her to show up in a black bodycon dress and formal boots.

Her makeup was lighter than usual, but the witch still made sure to paint her lips red. Margaret's eyes went wide as she took in the sight before her.

"Who are you?" she stammered.

"You were her sunset. But I am her Dawn," the witch said. "And I'm not going to let her go."

And with that, Summers pulled me back out into the main event space, shielding me from prying eyes and giving me a tissue. Today was a great day to wear waterproof and smudge-proof makeup, it seemed. God was merciful to me when I checked my compact and found I wasn't a total mess.

"Easy now. I'm here. I'm here," Dawn said. And when Margaret attempted to approach, the witch just smiled devilishly and pulled me out onto the dance floor where she spun me and showed off a surprising amount of formal dance training.

When I could breathe again and speak coherent sentences, I asked, "What are you doing here?"

The witch looked into my eyes and said, "Well, I'd intended to surprise you. But when I saw Margaret making her move, I decided to intervene when she wouldn't take a hint."

"How did you get in?"

She grinned.

"Kitchen entrance. Offered one of the cooks a blunt, and he was suddenly much more open to smuggling me inside."

This girl is unbelievable, I thought.

We continued to dance, and Margaret eventually sighed and left us alone.

"How much did you overhear?" I finally asked.

Dawn slid her hand further down my waist.

"Enough to make a grand entrance."

I snorted and we narrowly avoided bumping into an elderly couple who gave us a right evil stare. Dawn, in all her sophistication, stuck her tongue out at them. And they made guffawing noises, leaving the dance floor altogether while the symphony continued to play.

Suddenly, I didn't care why or how Dawn got here. I was just overjoyed that she'd showed up to surprise me. And I suddenly remembered her words.

"She's with me now," the witch had said with all the surety in the world. And that sent nothing but warmth and goodness through my entire body.

I looked deep into her emerald eyes.

"Hey, Dawn?"

"Yes, FeeDee?"

"Am I. . . with you?" I asked.

Without hesitation, she quietly asked, "Aren't you?"

I nodded.

"I want to be."

"Then you are. You're with me."

We stopped dancing, and I finally did something I'd wanted to do for weeks but never found the courage for. I pulled Dawn's face forward, and our lips locked. I ran my fingers through her hair, and the witch shivered.

When we parted, a few more people were staring, but nobody said anything. We went back to dancing and as a slow piece echoed out from the symphony, I rested my head on Dawn's shoulder, finally feeling like I was standing on solid ground for the first time tonight.

After a while, I asked, "So, what now?"

Dawn shrugged.

"I suppose we just keep dancing together."

"Because I'm yours?" I asked.

She giggled.

"Yes, FeeDee. Because you're mine."

17

(Dawn)

A lone cricket chirped in the dooryard as I stood at the front door of a home I'd been invited to days ago but had yet to enter. Sure, I'd been to the little guest house out back several times since FeeDee and I started "officially" dating. But the building before me was Casa de Ricci, the house of Franky Jr. and Bianca.

No biggie, I thought. *Just about to have dinner with your girlfriend's parents.*

I smoothed the purple dress I was wearing and pushed back my loose curls.

"What's to worry about?" I whispered to myself. "I've talked with Frankie Jr. plenty of times in the newsroom. This is just like that, except we'll be eating dinner. And his wife and two daughters, one of whom I'm now regularly kissing, will be at the table with us."

A rustling in the bushes caused me to jump as my girlfriend walked around the house.

I might have made an embarrassing yip, but it was quickly followed by a sizable scowl.

"You are so cute, you know that?" Frankie asked as I crossed my arms. "I've been watching you panic for about two whole minutes now. I was tempted to see how long you'd stand there, except I know Mamma just pulled her lasagna out of the stove and is waiting to meet you."

Heat crept over my cheeks.

"You were just standing there watching me?!" I asked. "And did you just say 'Mamma'?"

Frankie stepped closer and lightly ran her fingers down my cheek, which chased some of the grumpiness away.

"I couldn't help it. You were just so pretty highlighted by the window lights. And it's the only time I've ever seen you unsure about something. So. . . y'know. . . I couldn't pass that up. I had to observe for as long as I could," Frankie said. "And, yes. Things. . . are a little different during family dinners. You'll see."

My scowl only deepened despite Frankie's proximity.

"I'll give you a pass on the family nicknames thing. But with regards to spying on me, you know I'm a witch and could hex your ass, right?"

"No you won't," she said.

I raised an eyebrow.

"So sure, are we?"

"Yup. I remember reading your column yesterday about observing The Rule of Three, so I'm not too worried about you hexing me."

"Fuck," I hissed before she kissed me and scattered any remaining curses away.

Y'know, there was a time when being a witch meant people feared you, I thought before Frankie chased that grumpy thought away as well.

A few minutes later, I was seated across from Frankie at a long oak dining table that could comfortably seat eight people. Tonight, it would hold five.

My eyes darted up to a little crucifix hanging above the doorway, and it was hard for me not to squirm.

Easy now. They're the chill kind, I thought.

A dimmer switch sat next to a large china cabinet filled with expensive-looking dishes. Long blue curtains hung over a window on the next wall.

The table before us was already set with cloth napkins and what appeared to be antique cutlery. I imagine if I'd asked, Frankie Dee would tell me her great-great-grandmother came to Maine and walked off the boat with nothing but the dress on her back and a small box of this very silverware.

Lit candles provided most of the light with the dimmer switch apparently set to "mood lighting." A warm golden glow fell over Frankie, and I realized this was maybe the first time I'd ever seen her in comfortable clothes.

My girlfriend sat across from me wearing a sweater and leggings. Her hair was pulled back in a lazy bun. Frankie looked like she'd hopped out of the shower not too long ago.

Franky Jr. walked into the dining room carrying a basket of seasoned bread wrapped in a thin red cloth. It smelled heavenly.

"Hey! It's my favorite witch. Good to see you again," he said with the warmest inflection I'd ever seen. I awkwardly shook his hand before Frankie Jr. sat at the head of the table.

My girlfriend just shook her head and said, "Don't mind Papà. He's always excited just before dinner time."

Relatable, I thought. *Also. . . Papà?*

I pulled a bottle of wine out of my purse and handed it to the patriarch.

"Thank you for having me tonight," I said. "I'm excited to meet the rest of Frankie's family."

"Oh! That's very kind of you," he said, taking the bottle of wine and grunting as he stood up and walked into the kitchen. I could hear him talking with an older woman, likely Bianca. He was probably getting instructions on exactly which wine glasses to use. He re-entered with the bottle and a few stemmed glasses, placing them on the table.

Shifting in my seat, I watched Bianca waltz in behind her husband.

"Coming up behind you," she said, both hands holding a massive lasagna that was still steaming.

Bianca was around Frankie's height but a little more heavy-set. She wore a tiny pair of glasses on the bridge of her nose with her ashen hair tied back into a large braid.

Her red blouse and jeans were covered by a stained gray apron.

Frankie grabbed a potholder and tossed it on the table under Bianca's lasagna just before the matriarch set it down.

"Ah, thank you, FeeDee."

"That's a heavy one, ah?" Franky Jr. asked, waggling his eyebrows. "I hope your girlfriend brought her appetite."

He exchanged glances with Frankie as he said that, and my girlfriend snickered.

Bianca turned to my spot at the table, and it felt like a surge of gravity pulled me into her full gaze.

"Oh! You should have told me she'd arrived! Come here, dear. I'm so excited to meet you."

And suddenly, I was standing in Bianca's arms as she lightly kissed each of my cheeks.

"Such a pretty girlfriend," she said as Frankie buried her face in her hands. "I can see why my daughter is so taken with you."

"Okay, thanks, Mamma. You can let my girlfriend go now," Frankie said.

Bianca scoffed but still held me close.

"Always cranky, this one. But she hasn't brought another girlfriend home for months! 'I'm gay,' she tells me, which is fine. I love my sweet girl. But that's not an excuse to stay single for so long, ah? Love who you want, but I still want a grandbaby before we all move to Mars."

"Mamma!" Frankie scolded.

I giggled.

"Oh, I'm well acquainted with her crankiness. You should see how she behaves when the vending machine in the breakroom is out of chips. She takes it so personally! Like, baby, there's only so many slots for chips. The vending guy isn't doing this to make you mad."

Silence fell over the table, and for a moment, I worried I'd said something wrong. But then boisterous laughter and shouts filled the dining room as Franky Jr. yelled, "That's true! That's exactly how she is."

And Bianca let loose a husky chuckle before patting my cheek lightly.

"I like you," she said. "You're very pretty and already know my little FeeDee so well. I want you at my dinner table anytime you're hungry. Got that? You'll have a second stomach by the time I'm done feeding you."

Warmth spread through my heart as this invitation reached the most neglected parts of my inner girl. The little girl who lost her family as a teen and hadn't sat around a dinner table with one since emerging from the tiny corner she often hid herself in. And with one bold sweep of the sights before me, the small inner child beamed.

"You're not scaring me, Mrs. Ricci," I said with all the confidence and swagger I could muster. "Your food smells so good that I wouldn't complain if I had five stomachs after eating here."

Another husky laugh from my hostess covered the noise of Frankie's sister walking into the dining room.

"Hey! Looks like I'm just in time," a new voice said.

I knew from Frankie's stories that her younger sister was named Tina. She walked into the dining room wearing black pants and a white uniform shirt that said, "Great Day Spa."

The word "Owner" was embroidered in black thread underneath the store's name.

Franky Jr. crossed his arms and said, "Just in time? You're late! I had to set the table for you."

Tina laughed and said, "That's what I mean! Just in time. . . to avoid any chores."

Bianca walked over and kissed her daughter on top of her head.

"Tinaaaaa, you shouldn't make your father set the table! You know he has to take it easy with that heart of his."

Franky Jr. clutched his chest and made a show of grimacing in pain.

"Yeah, SweetTee. Your old man. . . can barely function with his poor broken heart. How could you be so cruel to your Papà?" he asked.

Tina rolled her eyes.

"Oh my god. Why don't you ever give my sister this much grief?" she asked, walking into the kitchen to wash her hands. She returned with side dishes in each hand, baked zucchini and honey-roasted carrots. Each smelled amazing.

I was fighting a mouth full of drool as I stared at more of this heavenly food.

Frankie hugged her sister and said, "Oh, they just give me grief before you arrive. It's been that way since I moved into the guest house. I thought I'd get less grief helping Papà after the heart attack, but somehow I got more."

Tina made her way over to me.

"You must be Dawn. I've heard so much about you!"

"And I can assure you, very little of it is true," I said.

Frankie's sister laughed and gave me a small hug.

"She warned me that you were funny. I hope Mamma didn't scare you off by mentioning grand-babies already."

Bianca locked eyes with me and shook her head behind Tina.

I just shrugged.

"Nope. Just kissed me on each cheek and welcomed a pagan to her table," I said.

The matriarch winked at me and sat next to her husband, leaning over and kissing him on the cheek. He smooched her back and then kissed her hand.

"My tesoro," he said, kissing her fingers a second time.

Tina ignored them and raised an eyebrow at me.

"Lying for Mamma already? Oh, she'll love you. You're going to fit in well at this table," Tina said, taking a seat and laughing.

With everyone seated, I got the sense from my family meals growing up that this was when they'd bless the food. Delicious food. Steaming food. Perfect, mouthwatering food. My gods, it was just begging to be catapulted into my stomach. The melted cheese on the lasagna, the flaky goodness of that buttered bread, the tender veggies waiting to slide onto my plate.

I had a hard time remembering when I'd last eaten a home-cooked meal that didn't come out of my own oven.

If I expected any strange looks before the prayer, I got none. They all knew I worshipped different gods and gave zero fucks about it.

All Franky Jr. asked was, "We're going to bless the food, but I know you have different beliefs. Would you prefer to step out for a moment while we pray?"

"Oh, no. I'm perfectly fine. Thanks for asking," I'd said.

He'd nodded, they all bowed their heads, said a few words of gratitude, and then I was shoveling the most delicious lasagna I'd ever eaten into my belly.

The basket of bread seemed to multiply like it would feed 5,000 people, and that was the kind of miracle I could get on board with.

A few minutes into dinner, Frankie turned to her father and said, "Oh, before I left the newsroom today, I got our latest subscription numbers."

His eyes perked up.

"Oh yeah?" he asked as silence fell over the table.

My girlfriend nodded.

"Dawn's new audience paid off. Our numbers are up four percent after seeing declines for the last few quarters."

I beamed at the news. And Frankie reached across the table to take my hand as I congratulated her.

She turned to Franky Jr. to see his reaction, and the patriarch looked like he couldn't believe it. His smile was all cheer and wonder.

"Really? The Lighthouse-Journal's audience grew this last quarter?" he asked.

Frankie took a bite of her bread and nodded. She had a big smile plastered on her face.

"You really swooped in and helped put some

wind in our sails," the journalist said, looking at me again, which just left me rubbing my feet together in glee. It was impossible to stop the small grin on my face from growing.

Her father nodded and took a drink of the wine I'd brought.

"That's a good start. Think you can keep working your magic into the next quarter?" he asked, winking at me.

"Oh, I don't plan on going anywhere," I said, sending my own wink across the table at Frankie. She nearly choked and took in a desperate gulp for air.

Franky Jr. laughed and slapped the top of the table.

"She really does have you twisted into pretzels, FeeDee," the patriarch said.

"Let's not do this now, Papà," she said, hiding her mouth behind a napkin.

He grinned in a way that said we would absolutely be doing this now. Then, I was the center of his focus again.

"All I'm saying is it's funny, ya know? I've known people who got together with their bosses in order to get a job. But Dawn, you did the exact opposite! You got the job to get with your boss," he said, pounding the table and laughing.

"Papà!" Frankie hissed while staring daggers at him.

Now Tina was laughing in between bites while

Bianca just smiled politely and watched the drama unfold.

As my girlfriend's cheeks heated, all I could do was beam. This family really seemed to like me, and that went counter to all the horrible scenarios that played out in my head as I'd stood frozen on their front porch earlier.

Tina's voice brought me out of my thoughts.

"So, Frankie tells me you've got a podcast?"

I nodded.

"I do! It's called Dawn's Divinations. I talk tarot, discuss the latest star movements, and have guests on to discuss their new witchy books or songs they've written. It's a lot of fun but also a lot of work managing it all."

The younger sister nodded.

"And Frankie says you built it all yourself! That's so cool. I love seeing women succeed at building their own businesses," she said, finishing her plate of mostly lasagna.

"Can I assume from your shirt that you own a spa?" I asked.

Tina looked down at her clothes.

"Whoops! Ha, yeah, I ran out of time to change before leaving. Had to cover an evening shift for one of my desk workers."

"Running a spa sounds challenging," I said. "I can't imagine what all goes into managing a brick-and-mortar business with clients."

Tina reached for another slice of bread.

"Oh, it's got challenges, for sure. Some days I want to pull my hair out. But then I remember that I built this place myself and that usually summons enough pride to swallow most of my grumbling. You should come by sometime! I'll give you a tour, and we can have a girls' day gossiping about FeeDee."

I tried to push back a tear as I realized this family was just eating me up. And. . . I hadn't been welcomed into a family for years now. You don't ever forget how long and quiet the holidays are when there's no warm table for you to sit around with loved ones.

When you take a heart that grew up with these things and starve it of family traditions and adoration, a part of it shrivels up. It's like a muscle that's no longer being used.

But sitting here, sharing a meal with Bianca, Franky Jr., Tina, and the girl of my dreams seemed to be breathing life back into that tiny piece of atrophied muscle.

There was love here. Real love. And to think that some of it would be directed my way left me suddenly ravenous for more. My stomach was full, but my heart wanted to eat up every ounce of love at this table without pause for thought.

So, with a deep breath and a stifled tear, I looked at Tina and said, "I'd love that. It sounds like fun."

FeeDee raised an eyebrow.

"Which part sounds like fun, Summers? The girls' day or the gossiping about me?"

That was a loaded question with 12,000 traps ready to activate, so I let Tina answer for me. She just grinned at her sister and said, "Yes."

AFTER DINNER, we said our goodbyes. I was given a bag of leftovers that found their way into FeeDee's kitchen. We'd walked through the backyard and into the guesthouse that made up her living space.

"So you moved in here to help your father after his heart attack?" I asked while Frankie opened her own bottle of wine and poured us each a glass.

She nodded.

"I was so scared that I was going to lose him if I let the man out of my sight. And Mamma works part-time at a restaurant in town, so she was going to need an extra hand one way or another. They didn't even ask. I just broke my lease and moved in one weekend."

"That's very sweet of you," I said as we sat on Frankie's couch.

My girlfriend shrugged.

"Yeah, well, I'm not exactly in a hurry to rush back into the death trap that is Portland's rental market. The apartment I left was $2,000 for one-bedroom. And they raised the rate to $2,300 after I moved out. When I first moved in, it was a decent deal for $1,300 a month. But they just kept raising the price every time I renewed my lease. And it's not like the apartment got any better to live in. I didn't get anything extra for my money."

I groaned.

"Eat the rich," I said.

"If I wasn't full of Mamma's lasagna, I probably would."

We both laughed at that.

After we watched a few episodes of *Brooklyn 99*, both of us checked our phones.

"Are you staying the night?" Frankie asked.

I looked at my third glass of wine and downed it.

"Sure looks that way, FeeDee. Unless you want me to Uber back to my place and have you drive my car to pick me up before work tomorrow."

She shook her head.

A thick tension suddenly filtered through the room, and I felt nothing but fire as I stared into my girlfriend's honey-stained eyes. Despite the fact that we'd been dating for a few weeks now, we'd yet to actually bone, a fact that was not lost on us at the end of each night.

It wasn't like we'd specified ground rules about how and when we'd get intimate. I think we'd just been carrying all this sexual tension after our first night together, a night where we almost. . . and then Frankie put up these professional boundaries.

Now, we were finally together. And it wasn't like

we'd been entirely chaste. But we'd yet to actually have sex.

We'd fallen asleep together quite a few times. But I hadn't even seen Frankie's panties.

And that was fine! I wasn't in a rush. We clearly had something good here, and I didn't want to fuck it up by fucking too soon.

Of course. . . I'm only human. Tonight, both of our inhibitions lowered, and we'd just finished the episode where Holt meets Rosa's girlfriend, Jocelyn. Things were a little steamy in my mind and based on how many times Frankie's fingers had found ways to brush over my tits in the last half hour, I think it was safe to say her body was cooking on the same level mine was.

So, we brushed our teeth. I took a quick shower, unable to stop wishing she was in there with me. And the two of us found ourselves sitting on opposite ends of FeeDee's mattress. While I chewed my thumbnail, Frankie absentmindedly scratched the back of her head.

Why was this so difficult? We'd spent all this time and energy trying not to have sex after almost doing it once, and now it felt like there was no natural segue back to the land of moans and orgasms, also known as the Lesbian Promised Land.

You know what? I thought, feeling my need to absolutely ravish this woman rise to the surface. *I'm tired of pretending like our relationship is made of glass.*

"Hey, FeeDee?" I asked.

"Yeah?"

"Wanna fuck?"

My girlfriend's eyes sparkled, and I thought, *Yeah, she's hungry for it too.*

"Why did it take so long for one of us to ask?" she pondered, scratching her head.

I shrugged and stared at one of the many framed newspaper clippings FeeDee had decorating her walls.

"We were both scared of breaking what we'd waited so long to have that neither wanted to take the risk," I said.

The newspaper editor nodded.

"Then. . . what changed? Why ask tonight?"

I grinned and said, "Because I'm horny as fuck, and I'm pretty sure my period is going to start this weekend. So. . . perfect timing, really."

Rolling her eyes, my girlfriend giggled before running a few fingers down her thigh. That hungry stare reappeared in her eyes so effortlessly. Did she know how sexy she looked doing that? Could she summon those eyes at will? I took a deep breath and chased those questions out of my mind.

"Are you still worried I'll fall asleep on you again?" Frankie asked, suddenly clutching invisible pearls.

As I crawled across the mattress to my girlfriend, I whispered, "I don't plan for you to sleep until you've shouted my name loud enough for everyone on Peaks Island to hear."

Frankie lowered her lips until they were an inch from my own. Her eyes searched mine, and time seemed to stand still between us.

She whispered, "Make me."

The defiance in her tone summoned an animal-like snarl from my lips as I nudged the newspaper editor back against her headboard, quieting any doubt she might have had about my ability to make her scream. I think we both knew at this point that she'd get there and by no one's hands but my own.

I brought my mouth together over her bottom lip and bit it, eliciting a small hiss of pleasure from my girlfriend. Pulling away just long for Frankie's face to contort into an expression that said, "Get your ass back here," I returned my lips to hers with renewed possession.

She pulled me into her lap as I pushed ahead, shuffling my hands in Frankie's hair, pulling her bun loose so I had something to run my fingers through.

"Yeah?" she whispered.

"Mmmhhmmm," I responded before kissing Frankie again and tangling our tongues together to elicit a soft moan from my girlfriend's throat.

Her noises made me positively wild, and I suddenly had to get that sweater off her body. With one quick motion, it fell to the floor, and I was staring at Frankie's breasts, pert and ready to be my playthings.

"I want you to make some noise, sweetheart," I said.

"Then get to work so — ohhhhhhhhh, my god," she said, starting sassy and involuntarily transitioning to a guttural noise as I fondled her tits with my now-free hands.

I grinned as warmth continued to build in my core.

"Yeah?" I asked, teasing and continuing to rub my thumbs over her stiffening nipples. "How's that? Am I getting to work?"

She nodded, falling short of any discernible words.

"Maybe I should work a little harder?" I whispered in Frankie's ear. She shivered as my teeth scraped against her neck.

I ran my tongue over one of her nipples before lightly biting it.

"Ahhhh," Frankie uttered.

"That's a good girl. I'll bet your panties are already soaked, aren't they?" I whispered.

She didn't respond with words. Or maybe she just couldn't, eyes fluttering as I fondled my girlfriend for another minute.

I rose for a second to pull Frankie flat on the bed and peel down her leggings. A black pair of bikini panties with a tiny pink bow in the center greeted me.

Tracing my fingers over the soft cotton, I felt Frankie squirm.

"I was right. You are wet," I said, eager to finally taste my girlfriend.

I continued to play with Frankie and tease her, running my fingers over her underwear, occasionally sliding under. She only grew wetter.

When Frankie's eyes betrayed her pressing need, I giggled mischievously. Judging by her stares and the widening of her legs, my girlfriend was positively desperate for what I offered. That only drove me all the more wild as I licked my lips. Desperation was intoxication at this moment, even more than the bottle of wine we'd finished.

I slipped a hand into my girlfriend's underwear, finding just the right angle. Frankie was beyond ready as my fingers entered her.

Pushing a little deeper, I watched Frankie's eyes close and flutter as I worked her.

"God," she hissed, like it'd been an eternity since she'd been touched.

"No, my sweet. Tonight you worship at my altar," I said, sliding another finger inside.

With a shiver and a moan, Frankie rode my fingers, and I worked them into a curved, truly wicked rhythm. Watching her face closely, I tailored my touch to drive her right up to the edge.

Frankie's hands grabbed the edges of my dress and pulled tight.

"That's it," I said, continuing to press forward.

Without warning, my girlfriend keened, pleasure consuming her entirely as her hips bucked.

"Oh god. . . I'm about to come, Dawn."

"Do it, then. Come for me, Frankie."

Her body shuddered as she called my name, voice echoing through the bedroom as though ripped from Frankie's lungs.

And then she came, taking short breaths that transitioned to whimpers like some sort of chemical reaction.

"All the magic in the world, and all that's required to turn you into putty between my fingers is. . . well, my fingers, it turns out," I grinned.

It took about half a minute for Frankie to find her words.

"You don't have to. . . be so smug about it," she laughed. "You look like the cat that ate the canary."

I laughed.

"FeeDee, I'm about to eat more than just the canary as soon as you catch your breath."

Her eyes widened.

"You expect me to bounce back that quickly?"

"I don't know about bouncing, but I expect you'll be shaking again soon enough."

Before she could retort, I hooked my girlfriend's knees in my elbow and pulled her down further on the bed. She honest-to-god yipped. And when I pulled down her soaked panties? Nothing but a blissful sigh.

I put my mouth to work, kissing and licking Frankie Dee as her hands flew to the comforter and squeezed tight.

My tongue entered Frankie softer than silk.

"Fuck!" she gasped as my fingers took over for

my tongue, curling and pressing against Frankie's wall.

I closed my mouth over her clit, sucking, licking, and sucking some more.

The newspaper editor's fingers flew from the comforter to my hair, pulling tight, and then pushing my head forward a little. Frankie's thighs quivered as she was clearly struggling to think, worry, or even form words.

"You taste so fucking good, do you know that?" I sighed, taking in every single ounce of what Frankie offered me.

I got back to work as Frankie moaned louder. Without a shred of mercy, my tongue lapped at the trembling woman beneath me.

All she could do was whimper and hiss my name.

It didn't take long for my girlfriend to break again. Her thighs tightened around my head, nails digging into my scalp, as she screamed at her ceiling fan, "Mary! Mother of God! Fuck!"

Nipping the inside of her leg before I lapped up more of Frankie's juices, I half-laughed/half-scolded, "Excuse me. My name is Dawn. Goddamn Catholics, I swear."

Giggling some more, I felt Frankie pull me up her body and kiss me, sharing in her juices that were still dripping down my chin.

"We'll work on your obscenities," I said, leaning down to kiss each of her breasts one more time.

She shivered a little more and then tried to catch her breath.

"Holy shit, Summers. That was amazing," Frankie said.

I cupped her cheek until she stared at me.

"You were the one who said 'make me.'"

My girlfriend grinned.

"I sure did, bub."

We snuggled for another minute in silence before the newspaper editor spoke again, a soft smile gracing her lips.

"For once, I'm well fed, well rested, and well fucked," Frankie said.

I giggled, stretching.

"Well, I'm happy to have contributed to that last one. I ate well twice tonight."

"You have, haven't you?" my girlfriend said in a flirting tone. "And now it's my turn."

Without warning, Frankie flipped me over.

"Since we've established that I've been well-fucked, I think it's your turn, Miss Witch."

"Oh yeah? Is that what you think?" I asked, feeling her weight on top of me and the fire in my core reigniting.

I wasn't a stone butch by any means, but I definitely enjoyed giving more than taking. With that said, if Frankie wanted to fuck me senseless, I wasn't opposed to it by any means.

"I always wondered why you wore so many dresses," Frankie said lifting my skirt to reveal a set of pink hipster panties. "And I suspect the reason is, you got fucked in a sundress once, and always wanted to be prepared in case it happened again."

"Right. It's not because I enjoy dressing femme. It's that I just have the feminine urge to get my pussy eaten while wearing a dress. You got me," I said, rolling my eyes.

But I lost all smugness when Frankie started to run her fingers over my underwear, teasing me as I did to her earlier. A whimper escaped my throat.

"And, as expected, you are positively soaked from earlier."

Before I could respond, she slid the panties down my legs and tossed them off the bed.

"Ah well. You won't be needing those for a while," Frankie said, licking her lips and adjusting my skirt, pushing it up all the way. "Wow. That is one gorgeous pussy."

Heat flooded my cheeks, and for once in my life, words failed me. I'm the person who always had a snarky remark, but tonight, I was disarmed.

Before long, Frankie's tongue licked up the center of my cunt, and I writhed on the bed as shivers of pleasure raced through me. I moaned and looked down at the gorgeous woman eating me out.

"Seems I'm not the only one who tastes good. You're goddamn delicious, Summers."

So, I lay there vulnerable and in the grasp of my lover as she built enthusiasm for the godsgiven perfection that is cunnilingus. I thanked Aphrodite for the many wonders of passion and Sappho for the many ways love is shared between women.

I was slick from fucking and fingering Frankie. But now I was on the receiving end as she lapped at me, paying close attention to my clit.

More tension built in my core as shivers of pleasure raced to every corner of my body, courtesy of my girlfriend's enthusiastic licking and sucking.

"Fuck," I moaned.

"Yes," she said between licks. "We certainly are."

If I made Frankie scream earlier, she seemed eager to return the favor now, and I was getting awfully close.

"Frankie," I hissed. "Frankie, gods, Frankie."

I gasped for air as all my bliss threatened to spill over into orgasm, to the point that I could hardly stand it. My eyes burst open as I shouted Frankie's name and arched my back.

"That's it, sweetie. Keep going. You're almost there," my girlfriend said before lowering her mouth back to my cunt.

I grabbed the blankets beneath me with everything I had and braced for the orgasm of the century.

"Damn, you really do taste good," Frankie said, continuing to lap at me.

All I could do was shiver in response.

Just before I lost all control, Frankie asked, "Who fucks you senseless?"

"You!" I hissed.

"And what's my name?"

"Frankie Dee," I yelled as my entire body shook and I came all over her face.

My girlfriend continued to lick and seemingly get every drop of me she could as I took ragged breaths and lay sprawled on the bed. The afterglow consumed me as my thighs got their final shakes out of my system.

At last, the newspaper editor collapsed beside me.

Neither of us spoke for a while until I asked, "You have a. . . washer and dryer in here, right?"

Frankie nodded.

"Okay, good. I'm going to need to wash. . . well, everything, in the morning before we leave."

"Or I could just loan you some clothes," Frankie said.

"Or you could just loan me some clothes," I repeated and curled up closer.

After we both got up for our nightly routines, we collapsed back onto the bed. It occurred to me that we were once again on the comforter.

"I'm too tired to climb under the covers," I mumbled.

Frankie nodded and reached down to the floor, bringing back a brown fuzzy blanket. She rolled onto her back and flicked it open a few times, using her tired legs to spread it over us.

"Gods, you're perfect," I smiled, as she scooted closer to me.

I didn't get a response and soon found it was because my girlfriend had fallen asleep almost as soon as the blanket touched us.

"Well, at least she waited until after the sex this time," I mumbled and closed my eyes, joining her in slumber.

18

(Frankie)

My fingers hovered over numbered buttons on the dial pad, gray circles on a lit screen that had the potential to drastically alter my immediate future. My heart hammered in my chest as I stared at the phone number. It was one I'd dialed several times across numerous visits. By this point, I had it memorized.

The idea of what I'd be told when I arrived some days or weeks from now left my hand shaking. But after spending part of this morning doubled over in my office, waiting for my chest pain to subside, I knew it was time. I couldn't keep ignoring this. Yes, Dawn would be furious with me if I did, but the truth was. . . I hadn't pulled up this phone number for my girlfriend's sake.

I couldn't put my thumb on what exactly had changed since our family dinner together, but my desires felt different. Normally, I did nothing but work or think about work. That had been my life since the heart attack and getting dumped by my almost fiancee. It was too hard to even consider the possibility that I might be able to repair the part of my heart that wanted love again.

And against all odds, I'd been given love again. Call it God's will, the universe's desire, fate, or just the random luck of a plucky witch I'd hired in the course of my work, but. . . now my thoughts strayed toward Dawn, spending time together outside of the newsroom, and realizing that maybe broken things can be put back together given enough time.

It was time that forced me to unlock my phone and punch in the numbers. Because I wanted more time, with Dawn, with my family, and with myself. All of my time had been given to the Lighthouse-Journal, and now for the first time in months, I realized that this place shouldn't have one hundred percent of my time. . . or eighty percent of my time. . . or seventy percent of my time.

Maybe all this chest pain was my body's way of telling me it was time to rebalance the scales of my schedule. I watched my father sink all of his energy into this newspaper, and he watched his father do the same thing. One died. One almost died. Here I sat with red flashing lights telling me that my train was on the same tracks. And for the first time in my life, maybe I'd found a train I didn't want to be on anymore.

But I had to be the one to make that call. Not

Dawn. Not Dad. Not my staff. Me. Frankie Dee Ricci. Dawn might have made me realize I needed to change my life, but I still had to be the one to make that change.

And before my shaking fingers hit the green dial button, it wasn't Dawn's face that came to my mind (nor her tits). It was Mr. Cutlow, the asshole who'd tried to buy my newspaper and throw it into his portfolio of publications being bled dry for what little profit they could produce.

What was it he'd said at the convention center?

"You're half his age, Ms. Ricci. But you're working twice as hard as my little brother. My guess? This newspaper you're fighting so hard to cling to is slowly killing you. I'd never presume to tell you how to live your life. But if I were in your shoes, I'd be asking if my family's business was worth dying for," the New Yorker had said.

What has the world come to when the CEO of an equity firm is giving me life advice? I thought, shaking my head. Still, regardless of how much he'd annoyed me since our first phone call, I couldn't help but realize there was something strangely honest about the way he communicated. That had to be a rare fucking quality for a man in his line of work.

He was chasing after the opportunity to devour my family's dream, but the man wasn't trying to pull any fancy tricks or underhanded maneuvers. It was a straight chase. And while I'd never expect a gazelle to respect the lion hunting it, I could at least acknowledge the way he handled his pursuit.

"Fuck it," I thought, hitting the dial button and waiting for a second.

A man's voice answered on the other end, saying, "Maine Cardiology Clinic, how can I help you?"

Outside my office, the police scanner was saying something about a wreck on I-295. I closed the door before I spoke.

"Hi, yes, my father is a patient of Dr. Mendoza. I was wondering if. . . she might be accepting new patients?"

"What's your father's name?"

"Franky Ricci," I said.

Clicks from a keyboard filtered into the call, and the man I spoke with asked me a few more questions to verify my identity.

"Dr. Mendoza isn't taking new patients right now, but. . . hang on," he said, voice trailing off for a moment. "Actually, I do see a note in your father's chart that she'd be willing to see immediate family members if the need arose."

I'd been holding my breath without realizing it (which probably wasn't good for my aching heart). With a soft hiss, I let the air out of my lungs.

"Well, the need arose. I've been dealing with some chest pain for a — well, I've been dealing with chest pain. I'd like to see her if she has an opening in her schedule sometime in the next few weeks."

The harsh reality was it might be months before she got me in. Maine is statistically the oldest state in the U.S. We've got a lot of geezers living in the Pine Tree State. And specialists were hard to come by, let alone free appointments for the few that were here.

And I was lucky to live in Portland where we actually had some specialists. Outside of here and Bangor, if you needed a specialist, you were going to be driving for a while, especially up in The County.

"If you're free this afternoon, Dr. Mendoza just had her 1 p.m. patient cancel. I could put you in. Will that work?"

Again, I'd been holding my breath.

"Yes! That'd be perfect."

"Do you have insurance?" the receptionist asked.

I nodded, even though he couldn't see me through the phone call.

"I do. Green Cross Green Shield."

He typed something else into the computer.

"Alright. Bring your ID and insurance card, and we'll see you at one o'clock," the receptionist said.

I hung up and leaned back in my chair.

Holy shit, I thought. *What luck. Or . . . divine providence? That's what a godfearing Catholic is supposed to say, right?*

Staring at the bracelet Dawn had given me, I thought for a moment.

"Maybe it was just good luck from a witch who loves me," I muttered.

THAT AFTERNOON, I was sitting on a thin sheet of paper stretched over a long uncomfortable bed in Dr. Mendoza's examination room. The fluorescent lights were giving me a headache. Or maybe it was the fact that I'd skipped lunch. Sometimes, progress was slow. I had to pick between a good diet and seeing my doctor today. I went with the latter.

I'd already had blood drawn, my breathing checked, and an EKG. My adrenaline was starting to spike as I waited for Dr. Mendoza to decide if I'd need another test.

She knocked on the door and walked back inside, looking at a laptop she carried.

Without saying a word, the doctor sat down on a red stool and tucked her legs onto its lower bar.

"Okay, Frankie. I've looked at your test results and determined two things."

My heart jumped from my chest into my throat, and I tried to steady my breathing. What was she going to tell me? Did I need surgery? Would I have to see several other doctors? The endless possibilities ran through my mind as time seemed to slow before she spoke again.

"First, you're a very stubborn girl and every bit your father's daughter."

I raised an eyebrow.

"Excuse me?" I asked, not angrily, just stunned at her frown and agitated tone.

"You had chest pain but chose to wait two months to say anything about it! This could have been addressed when you brought your father here a few weeks back," she scolded. "I specifically asked you about your heart, and you said, 'Nothing to report, bub.' In case you were wondering, this is something you were supposed to report, BUB!"

I flinched. I knew I deserved this, but it still stung.

"I'm. . . sorry," I said, scratching the back of my head. "I got wicked dumb."

Dr. Mendoza scowled at me.

"I'll say! Here's your first diagnosis. You've got Stupid Fever."

I snorted.

"This isn't funny, Frankie. You could have wound up in the hospital like your father. And do you have any idea the stress it would put on his recovering heart if he knew you were in the ER? You could have derailed his entire recovery."

Clamming up, I cleared my throat and nodded.

"Yes, Dr. Mendoza. Sorry."

She stared at me until I felt her judgment finally subside. Looking back at her laptop, the doctor hit a few keys and rubbed her chin.

"Thankfully, you haven't had a heart attack,"

she said. "And you did finally wise up and book an appointment."

I sat waiting for her second diagnosis, the one that could hopefully be treated because God knows stupid has no cure.

The doctor sighed.

"What you do have is called stable angina. It causes intermittent chest pain, sometimes dizziness, and pain radiation down the neck or arm," she said. "Treatment is pretty straightforward. I'm going to send two prescriptions to your pharmacy. One is nitroglycerin tablets. You'll take them sublingually, one tablet every five minutes until your chest stops hurting. You can take up to three. If your chest doesn't stop hurting after three, you go to the ER."

I nodded.

"The other prescription I'm going to give you is called isosorbide mononitrate. You'll take that daily."

My brain finally clicked on one of the words I'd heard her say, and I grinned.

"Did you say nitroglycerin? Am I at risk of exploding if I take that?" I asked, giggling.

That scowl swung back my way, and Dr. Mendoza whispered, "Does this seem like the right time to be joking?"

A chill raced through my blood, and I took a slow breath. Outside the door, a nurse rolled by some kind of heavy cart that rattled the frame and my bed.

"No. Sorry, doctor."

Dr. Mendoza closed her laptop. She stood and set it on a nearby counter before popping her hip.

"Medicine is only part of the treatment," she said. "The other piece comes from you making better choices in your life. Eat three meals a day. Healthy meals, with vegetables and fruit. Cut back on the chips, you hear me, Frankie? And for God's sake, get eight hours of sleep every night."

I nodded. Dad was going to give me so much shit for all the things I scolded him for, only to now be in a similar position.

"And finally. . . I want you to take some time off work," she said. "Your body desperately needs rest. You've pushed it as far as it can go. Time to dial back for a bit."

"How long?" I asked.

She looked at a calendar on the wall.

"Let's say two weeks to be safe. You come see me again in two weeks, and we'll discuss getting you back in the newsroom. But Frankie, you need to listen to me. If you don't take this seriously, it'll only get worse. The only way you resolve this is with a full commitment to the treatment plan."

With a deep sigh, I expected disappointment to come. But instead. . . I felt. . . relief? How was that even possible? If I'd been told to take even a day off work last week, I'd have stormed out of the office and run myself ragged just for spite. But now? Things were different. I was different.

"Okay. I'll see you in two weeks, doctor. Thanks for all your help today."

She raised an eyebrow.

"I thought you'd fight me on this. What happened to the headstrong girl who charged into overnight shift after overnight shift regardless of the physical toll?"

I shrugged.

"I guess the fever broke."

Dr. Mendoza sized me up. And silence filled the exam room. After a minute of thinking, she picked up her laptop and opened the door to go.

"See you in two weeks, Frankie. Good luck."

━━

AFTER PICKING up my prescriptions at the pharmacy, I returned to the newsroom with some flutter of hope in my chest. It was like. . . my body sensed that it was going to get some rest and was releasing the few ounces of serotonin it had from a glass box labeled, "Break in case of good decision."

I sent a few emails and returned the phone call of a colleague I'd been wanting to meet with. We chatted for about half an hour, and I got a surprise invitation from him.

"Next week, then?"

"Yes. That sounds great. I'm looking forward to it." I said.

"See you then," he said.

I hung up and walked over to Isabelle's desk, eyeing her signed Boston Blue Sox ball sitting in its glass case. She was transcribing some notes.

Tapping her on the shoulder, I smiled when she looked up.

"What's up, Frankie?" she asked.

"Can I talk to you for a minute in my office? I've got a favor to ask."

She slid off her headphones and stood, clicking off the space heater under her desk. It didn't matter what time of the year it was. Isabelle had it running anytime her feet were parked there.

We walked into the office, and I closed the door, offering her a chair.

Isabelle didn't say anything, just waiting for me to speak. I sat down and sighed, a tiny shred of me still not wanting to have this conversation. But I squashed that tiny nerve like a gnat and turned to face the sports editor my father had hired years ago.

"How would you feel about taking the managing editor role for a little while?" I asked out of nowhere. Her eyes widened, and she fiddled with the sleeves of her blue blouse.

"What are you talking about?" she finally asked.

Clearing my throat and feeling a renewed weight in my chest, I pushed forward with a conversation where I did the one thing I hated more than anything else. . . I asked for help.

Old Frankie Dee wouldn't have done it. That bitch would just as soon have ignored her doctor's advice and charged straight ahead into certain doom, optimistic that she could weather the storm on her own.

But I wasn't the same old Frankie Dee. I was. . . moderately improved Frankie Dee, batteries sold separately because fuck you. No company is giving you free batteries. It'll cut into their profit margins by half a penny.

"Just got back from the doctor. She told me my heart is tits deep in the pucker brush. Gotta take a couple of weeks off to rest, swallow some pills, the works, bub. So I was wondering if you'd fill in for me while I'm gone. I'll find the money to make sure you're paid extra for the trouble."

"My god, are you okay, Frankie?"

I nodded.

"Yeah, I'm fine — er, I will be. Just gotta rest. I'll be back in two weeks. My Dad will still be here for a few hours most days if you have questions. And I'm just a text away," I said.

Isabella scratched her head.

"Who's going to run the sports desk while I'm you?"

"Pull Craig over. Tell him he's going to get some editor training. He's been itching for a chance to climb another rung on the ladder. Shit, he'll probably update his LinkedIn page again," I said, rolling my eyes. "He's got a good heart, though. Just gotta run all that puppy energy out of him. Let him cut his teeth on an editor assignment for a couple of weeks and see if that doesn't wear him out."

She nodded and rubbed her chin.

Outside in the newsroom, I watched Emma yelling at someone on the phone. I assumed she was bitching at a PIO for refusing to give her any details about a story. I snickered. That girl was doing a hell of a job here.

"What do we do about general assignments and breaking news if Craig is moving to the sports desk for a bit?" Isabelle asked.

She didn't seem panicked. The Latina had surprised me with how calm she was taking this shift. Maybe she was just relieved to see me finally stepping back to catch my breath. Who knows?

"Um, shit. I guess we could call over to Maine University South. Is Professor Kim still the faculty advisor for their college paper?"

"I think so," Isabelle said.

"Good. She can ask her journalism students if any of them want to freelance for us while Craig's off his normal beat. Hell, he may even have a friend or two he can recommend."

Emma slammed her phone down and yelled, "Fucking shitbag!"

Isabelle and I snickered.

"Who was she yelling at?" I asked.

My new managing editor shrugged.

"I dunno, but as soon as you get your ass home to rest, I'm going to walk over and find out. I could use some entertainment."

I smiled.

"Thanks for helping me. I know this is sudden."

"Sudden?" she asked, standing up. "No, trust me. We've all known you needed a break for a while now, Frankie. I'm just glad you're finally listening to someone and using up that pile of PTO I'm sure you've accrued."

The managing editor walked around the desk to put a hand on my shoulder.

"None of us wanted to see you end up like your father. He got lucky. And I'd just as soon advise you not to test that luck yourself. Though, when I consider your new girlfriend, I do find myself thinking you got lucky in your own way," she said, giggling.

My cheeks flushed, and I scoffed.

"If you're going to make inappropriate comments like that, I'll —" I started before Isabella interrupted me.

"Do jack shit," she said, finishing my sentence. "Because you're not the managing editor right now. You're an ornery 30-year-old who is being walked to the door and sent home to rest."

She grabbed my purse, threw it in my hands, and pushed me toward the door.

"I can't believe this is happening," I muttered,

stepping outside. "Is it too late to take it back? You've already gone mad with power."

Isabelle winked.

"Go rest. Those are your doctor's orders and now your boss' orders. And in case you've forgotten in the last five minutes, that's me. I'm the boss now."

With a chuckle and a knowing smile, I watched the new managing editor close the door to my newsroom, and I was left standing there feeling a little numb.

"Yup. Mad with power," I mumbled, walking to the sidewalk.

And instead of going home as I'd been ordered, I found myself looking up at the Portland Observatory, standing tall over me. Shrugging and realizing I had nothing but time to kill now, I decided to walk inside and (slowly) climb to the top, staring out over the city I'd busted my ass (and heart) informing.

My eyes moved from downtown to out over the harbor where a cargo ship was slowly entering the port with a couple of smaller boats helping it navigate the channel.

Leaning against the white wooden railing, I took a deep breath, held it, and let it go. A pair of seagulls flew next to the tower, and one of them shit on a guy walking below and staring at his phone.

"Are you fucking kidding me?!" the guy bellowed as I grimaced and moved to a different side of the observatory.

Tough luck, I thought. *Been there.*

I wasn't sure how long I stood looking out over the houses of Munjoy Hill, and beyond that, the bay. But hey, what did it matter? I was on vacation now, right?

Eventually, I heard footsteps behind me, and a voice I'd grown to truly love said, "Isabelle texted me to come and take you home. She said you were hiding in the observatory and pouting."

I laughed loudly and spun to kiss my girlfriend.

"Hi," I said.

"Hi yourself," she said, grinning. "So imagine my surprise when I'm scheduling a Zoom interview for tomorrow's podcast, and Isabelle tells me you need to be dragged home. Wanna tell me what that's about?"

With my back leaned against the railing, I took a deep breath and prepared to come clean to my girlfriend. I'd been taking a lot of deep breaths today. Maybe Dr. Mendoza was full of shit, and I was secretly fine. What if Isabelle knew I'd promote her temporarily, and she paid my dad's cardiologist to put this whole plan in motion? Eh, that's too indirect for her. If she wanted me gone, the woman had already proven she could physically remove me from the premises.

"Okay, I have a confession to make," I started.

"FeeDee, stop. You don't have to tell me you're secretly gay. I think the whole world knows at this point. Gods know you've enjoyed me tonguing your cunt way too much to be keeping up the ruse of a straight girl."

I froze. And before I could stop it, my mind began to replay those scenes of Dawn doing exactly what she'd said.

"No! C'mon, stop. I'm trying to be serious here. I went to the doctor today," I said, fighting my mind for control over the two brain cells worth of focus I had right now.

All of the joking expressions drained from my girlfriend's face.

"Are — are you okay?" she asked.

I nodded and took her hands in my own.

"Listen. The doctor said my heart is a little fucked up. She gave me some drugs and said I needed to take a couple of weeks off work. You were right. I. . . haven't been taking good care of myself. But! I promise I'm going to start. Here and now."

Dawn paused and waited for me to say more. When I didn't, she rubbed her thumbs over the backs of my hands.

"I'm. . . torn."

"Between?" I asked.

"Scolding you for ignoring this problem for so long and congratulating you on actually listening to someone and finally taking a break," Dawn said with a moody frown.

I groaned.

"Please don't. I already got chewed out by Dr.

Mendoza, and I'm tired. Besides, I have a surprise for you to make up for being an idiot."

"We've been dating for less than a month, and we've already hit the point where you're bribing your girlfriend to avoid being scolded for bad behavior?"

"Hey, by date number three we should have been married under the Lesbian Charter of 1975. We're already way off track, to begin with. My bribing you is just one more step down the path," I said.

Dawn rolled her eyes.

"Just, get on with the bribing before I remember that I'm mad at you."

Reaching into my purse, I pulled out my phone and showed Dawn an email.

"Amtrak tickets?" she asked.

A giddy surge shot through me.

"Yup! I bought us roomettes on two different trains."

My girlfriend's eyes widened as the wind picked up and blew my ponytail around like a fan blade.

"Trains? Plural? Where are we going?" she asked.

"Well, what better way to make sure I rest than by sticking my ass on a cross-country train?"

Dawn took all of this in and then nodded.

"Checks out. Again, though, where are we going?"

"Salt Lake City," I said. "On Saturday, we'll

take the Downeaster to Boston and hop on the Lake Shore Limited to Chicago. We'll stay a night there. Maybe eat some of that famous pizza they've got. Or was it the hot dogs they're famous for. . . anyway! The next day, we'll ride the California Zephyr to Utah."

The witch just shook her head while mouthing, "Wow."

Another few seagulls went screaming by. Summer was coming, and that made them extra feisty.

"If this is too sudden for you, I'll understand. And I got flex tickets, so if you want me to cancel, I absolutely can and get my money back. But I thought this could be a really fun trip for us. I've never stayed in a sleeper car before on a train, and this route supposedly has the best view of any Amtrak route in the country since it goes through the Rockies."

Dawn just giggled and pulled my hands up to her lips so she could kiss them. She thought for a moment while I waited for her answer.

"You're so fucking cute when you hyperfixate on your trains, you know that?"

I frowned.

"Don't tease me about trains! They're fucking awesome."

The witch laughed louder and nodded her head.

"Yes, FeeDee. They're awesome. And yes, I can

go. It sounds like a lot of fun. And, hey, we can join the — shit, what's the train equivalent of the Mile High Club?"

Hands flying to my belly, I laughed like there was no tomorrow. Except there would be a tomorrow. And a day after that. And another after that. Days I looked forward to living, truly living, instead of just working them away. I'd spend those days with a magical girl who'd reminded me that I was worth being loved and that it was worth the effort to pause and find joy in the little moments of our time together.

She didn't care that my heart had been broken physically and emotionally. Dawn spun a spell and put it back together with her witchy ways. Her real magic hadn't been in convincing me to stop working myself to death. No, the real magic was in showing me that I had the power to make that decision on my own and giving me the space to realize I wanted to make that choice.

I'd chosen myself. I'd chosen us. I'd chosen a future where I believed there was still plenty of magic to be found. And the next leg of that journey would come via locomotive.

"So. . . what's in Salt Lake City anyway? Are we converting to Mormonism because I don't think they handle lesbians very well," Dawn said. "Certainly much worse than Catholics."

I shook my head.

"I'm going to meet with the publisher of the

Salt Lake City Herald. It's one of the biggest newspapers out West, and a few years ago, amid financial turbulence, they transitioned from a for-profit news model to a nonprofit news organization. Their publisher said he'd give me a tour and walk me through how everything went."

"And that. . . saved their newspaper?" Dawn asked.

"It certainly helped. As a nonprofit, their organization can receive tax-free donations to fund their reporting efforts. Kind of like how the radio station Emma used to work at operates. They can organize fundraisers each quarter, and members pay to support the product. I think that model might just help save the Lighthouse-Journal."

My girlfriend narrowed her eyes and crossed her arms.

"That sounds suspiciously like work, FeeDee."

I spun to meet her argument head-on.

"No way! It's just a tour and some talking. That's not even close to work. I think you should congratulate me for my self-growth in being able to recognize that I had a problem and took steps to rest and fix it," I said, positively beaming with pride.

Dawn snorted and sauntered closer, pushing a strand of hair away from my face and tucking it behind my left ear.

"You're right. We should celebrate your retirement from being a career workaholic. Why don't you come back to my place, and I'll eat dinner. Maybe afterward, we can order takeout."

My face flushed, and I felt myself stammering as my head tried to recalibrate from once again being shortcircuited by the witch.

"Poor FeeDee. Been my girlfriend for weeks now and still get so easily flustered by my words. It's almost as adorable as when you ramble about trains."

"I hope you're ready to hear me ramble about trains for the entire trip west. I'll probably start with the retirement of the Amfleet cars before transitioning into a rant on why the Cascades route has a much easier journey over the Canadian border compared to the Maple Leaf or Adirondack."

Dawn lightly grabbed my chin and pulled me into a long kiss. When we parted, she licked her lips and whispered, "Can't wait."

And neither could I.

Afterword

Wow. So that's what it feels like to write a contemporary romance. Ashley Herring Blake and Meryl Wilsner make it look so easy! Phew. I'm tired. I really hope y'all enjoyed Frankie and Dawn. They were tons of fun to write.

I'm sitting here not long after my birthday and asking myself if I want to write another contemporary romance novel. And the answer. . . is yes. This was too much fun to do it just once.

But I've been teasing a dark dragon romance to my Autumn-ites for the last few months, and if they don't get it soon, I'm legit worried they'll feed me to Godzilla.

And for those of you who are waiting to find out what happens next to Sierra, my little bratty were-wolf, rest easy. Once I've finished writing about sapphic dragons, I'll bring you amazing readers back to Faerie. After that? Who knows! (Just kidding. I know. But I can't tell y'all just yet. You'll have to wait until the next Afterword to find out more.)

Okay, I've gotta get busy with some more formatting, and it's already midnight. That'll be all for this note. Thanks for reading my books!

In the meantime, watch more Godzilla movies! Buy and enjoy a box of donuts (gods, I wish Maine had Krispy Kreme). Ride your bike to the water, and check for mermaids.

Later, bub

- Autumn

About Autumn

Autumn Wolff is a Mainer, bub. And she's a woman of few simple interests. When she's not writing stories about girls kissing each other, Autumn is likely reading stories about girls kissing each other, playing Dungeons and Dragons, riding her bike, or watching a movie. She and her wife live near the ocean and consume more pizza than four turtles mutated by ooze. Autumn may not have the biggest living space, and it may never have enough book-shelves, but it's home.

Other books by Autumn

My Aunt, The Vampire

Heart of the Wolf Goddess

www.ingramcontent.com/pod-product-compliance
Lightning Source LLC
Chambersburg PA
CBHW021940120726
47992CB00001B/68